EDMUND+OCTAVIA

The Dulcie Chambers Museum Mysteries

by Kerry J Charles

An Exhibit of Madness
(Previous title: Portrait of a Murder)

From the Murky Deep

The Fragile Flower

A Mind Within

Last of the Vintage

FROM THE MURKY DEEP

A Dulcie Chambers Museum Mystery

Kerry J Charles

EDMUND+OCTAVIA

Cover Image: *Boats at Sea, Saintes-Maries-de-la-Mer*, 1888, Vincent van Gogh. This image is in the public domain.

ISBN: 0989457656
ISBN-13: 978-0-9894576-5-1

To the one who keeps me sane
and always brings me fruit. LYT

CONTENTS

For me, painting is a way to forget life.
It is a cry in the night, a strangled laugh.
~ Georges Rouault

CHAPTER ONE

He liked to run with his mouth open and his tongue hanging out on the left side. The kid took him to the beach quite often, and he especially liked to run there. It was early today, still a little misty. He took off as fast as he could go, down the beach, tongue hanging as always, ears flapping.

"Hey, Jack! Waitup!" the kid yelled.

'*Nope!*' he thought.

When he got to Big Rock sticking up out of the sand, he stopped. Jack loved Big Rock. So many great smells. If he was lucky, maybe something crunchy to chew on. He sniffed and sniffed, drooling a little on the slimy seaweed. He heard the kid walking up behind him, humming and dragging a stick in the sand. The kid liked Big Rock too.

Jack nosed around the edge of the hard stone and into the water lapping up against it. No waves today, really. Not much. He sniffed again and sneezed, sending chilly seawater spraying out in front of him. He shook his head vigorously making his tags clatter. Jack liked that sound.

He nosed into the seaweed a bit more. Now that smell was interesting! Kind of like a person and rubbery at the same time. He stopped and snuffled into it.

The kid came around the edge of the rock behind him, still humming. Jack heard him stumble, stop, and then make a strange noise. It was loud, like a yell and a scream all mixed up. Then he heard feet thumping against the sand. *'Oh good! We're going to run!'* Jack thought. He turned and launched himself up the beach trying hard to catch up with the kid, who was still making that odd sound.

ᘓ

Detective Nicholas Black stood in the water looking down at the body. The photographer had just moved away. Nick had taken off his shoes and socks, and rolled up his jeans, but they were wet anyway. The mist had not yet burned off. It swirled around him, the rock, and the body lying in the water.

Nick heard heavy footsteps and a grunting sound behind him. "Stop being such a wimp, Johnson. Take your shoes off and get over here," he said, not even turning around.

"Yeah, well that's where you're wrong," muttered Adam Johnson and held up a pair of rubber boots, knowing full well that Nick didn't see them. Johnson groaned as he heaved himself down onto the sand. He took off his shoes and, rolling up his pant legs as best he could, shoved his feet into the boots. It took him several seconds to push himself up to a standing position again. "There we go," he said to no one in particular. He looked down and smiled at his work.

Johnson splashed into the water, managing to spray it onto the entire backside of his partner's jeans. Nick turned around with an annoyed look. "Do you mind?" he said.

Nick looked back at the body, encased in a full wetsuit and wedged against the large rock that jutted out of the sand. "What do you make of her?" he asked. First impressions counted. First impressions were the most important, and typically what people tended to forget.

"Quite fit," said Johnson. He leaned over and looked more closely. Without thinking, he stepped backward and began to kneel down. His bottom dipped into the ocean and one boot filled entirely with seawater. He jumped up, cursing.

Nick laughed. "That's the fastest I've seen you move in a long time!" he said.

"Damn cold water!" grunted Johnson. He leaned over without bending his knees this time. "Look at her scuba gear. Not new. Not rented either, I don't think. No markings like that. Either hers or borrowed from someone." He pulled out a pair of latex gloves from his pocket and snapped them on his hands. Gently he flipped her air gauge over to see the front. He looked up at Nick. "Empty tank. She ran out of air."

Nick kneaded the back of his neck. He'd been craning it at an uncomfortable angle to see everything he could without moving the body. "If it's her equipment, then she knows what she's doing. Strange that she would run out of air."

"Yeah. Agreed. Ready to move her?" Johnson asked. Nick glanced up at the beach and signaled to the photographer. She nodded.

"Yup. Emily's got all her pictures for now. Let's get a couple of these guys down here to help." He called to the uniformed police who had been skimming rocks on the glassy water. One of them let out a cheer as he counted eight skips. "Oooh, big winnah!" he heard another say. They all laughed and came over to where Nick and Adam Johnson were standing.

"Okay. Go time. Take off your shoes if you don't want to get 'em wet. Let's put her up on the sand," Nick said.

"Can we take the scuba gear off, sir?" one of the officers asked.

Nick looked at Johnson. "Guess we'll have to," Johnson said. "Just the vest with the tank and the weight belt. Leave the mask and flippers on if you can."

One of the officers moved forward and unbuckled the weight belt. He had trouble trying to get it off. "Yeah, that's too heavy for Larry," another policeman said. They all laughed.

Nick had seen this before. Death was unnerving. Death like this was especially difficult. Humor was the only way that many could deal with it. He let the laughter die down then cleared his throat. "Let's get the vest and tank off all in one go. Unfasten it in the front, pull out the arm closest to the rock, then roll her into the water more. Peel the vest off as she rolls over." They managed without too much difficulty.

Her body floated easily in the shallow water, buoyed by the wetsuit. She was face up now. Nick looked at her again before they put her on the stretcher to carry her up the beach. Calm. That was the word that jumped into his mind. '*She looks calm*,' he thought. How could anyone be calm when they run out of air?

The police slid the stretcher under her easily in the water and carried her up onto the beach. They lowered the stretcher to the sand. "Let's at least take off her mask and gloves to get a look," Nick said. The mask came off easily, and left only red indentations on her forehead and cheeks.

Johnson pulled off her gloves. "No sign of grabbing or scraping really," he said, looking at them closely.

"Check her fingers," said Nick, still looking at the marks on her face.

"Nothing that shows any kind of struggle," his partner replied. "Look at this, though. Interesting. Looks like a phone number."

Nick swiveled around to look at the hand that Johnson held up. His mind began to whir furiously. '*No*,' he thought, but he knew that number. Whose was it? How could he know it? He shoved his hand into his pocket and pulled out his cell phone. Quickly, he scrolled through his contacts. Then he froze. "Oh my god," he said.

"What? What is it?" asked Johnson dropping the woman's hand. It landed on the sand with a soft thud.

Nicholas Black held up his cell phone to show Johnson the number that he had just found.

"Well, I'll be," Johnson murmured.

ଓ

Dr. Dulcinea Chambers, "Dulcie" to those who knew her for at least five minutes, sat in a meeting with what she thought could be possibly the two dullest people in the world. They were droning on about file organizational systems for the museum's collections. Dulcie listened politely. As the director of the Maine Museum of Art it was her job to organize, oversee, follow through, make decisions.... She felt her cell phone ringing in her pocket. She'd turned it to "silent" mode so that it would only vibrate when a call came through. *'Damn,'* she thought. *'If only I could take it. It'd be the perfect excuse to get out of this meeting.'*

Dulcie looked at the two people across the table from her. When the one currently speaking stopped to take a breath, Dulcie quickly interjected, "You sound as though you have this well in order. Is there anything that you need from me at this point?" They both shook their heads. "Well then, let's go ahead with what you're proposing. It seems like a great solution and will make file searching lots faster." They both smiled and their heads bobbed happily up and down in agreement. "Keep me posted on the progress?" she added. Again, they nodded, and Dulcie stood. "Thanks for filling me in," she said and left. They had already begun talking again, ignoring her as she walked into the hallway.

Dulcie closed the door behind her with a sigh of relief. She reached into her pocket and pulled out her cell phone. "Huh!" she said out loud. "That's strange!" It read, "MISSED CALL: NICHOLAS BLACK." She checked her voicemail. No messages. Maybe he had dialed her by accident? She hadn't even remembered that he was still in her contact list.

Nicholas Black had entered her life several months before when the Maine Museum of Art's board chairman and chief benefactor, Joshua Harriman, had been found dead in his home. Nick and Dulcie had pieced together some unfortunate facts that had led to the arrest of the culprit. Although Dulcie and Detective Black had shared a very pleasant dinner together after the case was closed, she had not heard from him since.

Dulcie decided to call him, curious to see why he had contacted her or at least why he would still have her phone number. She quickly pressed the Call Back button on her phone.

Nick answered before the first ring had ended. "Dulcie," he said. "I mean, Ms. Chambers. Dr. Chambers."

She laughed. "Just 'Dulcie' is fine. Did you call me? I have your number listed but no message."

There was a moment of silence. "Um, yes I did." He paused, not sure what to say. He couldn't exactly blurt out that Dulcie's phone number was scrawled on the hand of a dead woman that he had just pulled out of the Atlantic. "I need to talk with you about something, but it's a little strange. Would you mind meeting me, as soon as possible?"

"Yes, of course," she replied. "You have me intrigued. I'm done for the day with my scheduled meetings, thankfully. You have no idea what a welcome relief talking with you would be."

"Don't be so sure about that," Nick said. He tried to make the comment sound lighthearted, but failed.

Dulcie was instantly concerned. "Do you have time now?" she asked. "Would you like to come to the museum, or meet somewhere else?"

"Somewhere else," he said quickly. "Can you be at Roaster's coffee shop on Commercial Street in about half an hour?"

"Yes, I can," she said nervously. "Does this have to do with the Joshua Harriman case?" She desperately hoped not. Dulcie had found it very difficult to reconcile her feelings toward his death. She hoped nothing would rekindle her anger and sadness.

"No, not at all. I'll see you in half an hour," he replied.

Dulcie checked the time on her phone then put it back in her pocket. She continued through the maze of hallways that surrounded the museum's public spaces until she reached her office. Leaving the door open, she sat at her desk and scanned through the schedule for the next day. Her assistant, Rachel, poked her head in. "How'd the meeting go?"

Dulcie rolled her eyes. "They have everything totally under control, as you can imagine. Our records are in good hands and will be absolutely thorough and complete. Beyond thorough and complete. Did I mention thorough and complete?"

Rachel giggled. Her curly brown hair bounced over her shoulders. "Better them than me!" she said.

Dulcie laughed and said, "Or me either! Rachel, I'm heading out for a meeting in a few minutes. I probably won't be done before we close so I'll see you tomorrow."

"Sounds good. Have a good evening!" she replied.

"You too," said Dulcie. With a quick wave, Rachel disappeared around the corner. Dulcie closed her laptop, slid it into her bag and slipped into her standard black blazer.

'*Hmmm,*' she thought. '*Nicholas Black. Now why didn't he ever really ask me out? I was sure he would after we had dinner that once. Maybe he thought I was too upset then.*' She paused after putting on her blazer, looking down at her petite frame in the outfit of the day. She was wearing a beige sheath dress with a black border at the hem and black leather pumps. *I suppose I could attempt to look a little less boring. Color in my wardrobe wouldn't kill me.* However, the thought of actually shopping put her off the idea once again. Dulcie detested shopping. Nothing ever seemed to fit quite right, and the lights in the dressing rooms always made her look like a corpse.

She shrugged her shoulders in resignation and picked up her tote bag. From their brief conversation it did not sound like her meeting with Nicholas Black would be much of a social call anyway.

When she stepped outside, Dulcie immediately took off her jacket. It was only a lightweight linen, but the August sun had been blazing down all day and the morning's wind was gone. She slowed her pace and thought, '*They'd better have iced coffee at the ready today.*' Everyone on the street seemed to be mimicking her, walking slowly in the heat.

She finally reached Roaster's and pushed open the heavy glass door. It took a moment for her eyes to adjust to the dim light inside.

Nicholas Black looked up as she came in, watching her blink several times. His heart lurched once, briefly. '*Get a hold of yourself,*' he thought. '*Don't be stupid. This is an investigation.*'

Dulcie spotted him in a booth, halfway through a cup of coffee. She quickly walked over and slid in opposite him. "Good to see you again," she said, smiling.

"You too, Dulcie. Really. I wish it could be under better circumstances."

Her brow wrinkled. "What do you mean?"

"Well, to put it bluntly," he glanced at his half empty cup, then said, "Oh, sorry!" interrupting himself. "Let me get you something." She started to protest that she could get her own but he was on his feet quickly. "No, let me get it. It's the least I can do after luring you here for something like this. What would you like?"

She smiled. Something about Nick always made her feel at ease. His voice was quiet and strong at the same time. "Iced coffee. Milk and sugar please," she said.

"Good. Be right back."

Dulcie watched Nick give her order and chat with the woman at the counter for a moment. '*He must come here often*,' she thought. Then she remembered that the police station was only a block or so away. *Bet this coffee is way better than what they have there.* She smiled, imagining those terrible coffee vending machines that squirted out various syrups into hot water.

Nick came back, sliding her iced coffee and a straw along the table to her, and replacing his own cup with a fresh one.

Dulcie took a long sip. "Perfect. Thanks! Now, you were saying…."

"Yes. It isn't pleasant." He took a deep breath. "A body washed on shore this morning. A scuba diver. Looks like she ran out of air."

"Good god, that's awful!" said Dulcie. "But, how can I help? I've done some diving, and I'm certified, but you must have people to do that for you."

Nick looked surprised. He hadn't expected her to be a diver. "No, we don't need any help from that angle at this point, but there is something else. We can't identify her yet, but we do have a lead. Kind of an unusual one." He had been spinning his cup around on the table somewhat nervously. He made himself hold the cup still and looked her squarely in the eye. "Dulcie, it seems that your cell phone number was written on her hand."

Dulcie squinted at him. "My number?"

"Yes," said Nick, "and I'm afraid, if you don't mind, I need to take your cell phone to check all incoming and outgoing calls." He looked slightly embarrassed.

Dulcie sat back in the booth and scrutinized him for a moment. Then she took a deep breath and shook her head slightly as if to clear away confusion. "Of course," she said and pulled the phone out of her pocket. "How long will you have it?"

"We'll try to finish with it quickly. I'm sorry. Do you have any idea who this woman could be?" Nick asked.

"No, but I might have a better idea if I knew what she looked like, perhaps."

Nick pulled out his own cell phone. He looked up at her. "Can you handle this? Pictures of a dead person?"

Dulcie swallowed hard. "Yes, I think so, if they aren't too graphic."

"No, mostly she looks like she's asleep." He handed the phone to her with a picture of a woman's face on the screen. Dulcie studied it. "Are there more?" she asked without looking up.

"Yes, you can scroll through."

Dulcie flicked through the images. Something looked familiar about the woman. She was probably about Dulcie's age. Had she been in the museum recently? Perhaps.

Dulcie took a long pull on the straw and gulped her coffee. Then she looked up at Nick. "She looks familiar. I can't place her, but I'm pretty sure that I've seen her before. Maybe at the museum?"

"That might explain the phone number. Do many people know your cell number?"

"It isn't public, but it certainly has been circulated enough. Quite a few people have it at this point."

"All right. Well, if you could just keep thinking and let me know if you remember anything else about her. I'll get your phone back to you as quickly as I can, hopefully by tomorrow morning."

"Thanks, I appreciate that. It's my lifeline, unfortunately." She looked at Nick curiously. "Is there anything else? It seems like I don't have quite the whole story."

He'd forgotten how quick and intuitive she was, and for a moment it caught him off guard. "Nothing that I can tell you right now," he said.

"Well then," she replied. She took one last sip of cold coffee and slid out of the booth. "I'll wait for you to get in touch? You can call me at the museum." He nodded. "Nick, there's nothing else you can tell me? It could help me remember something."

"I'm sorry, but I really can't say anything else right now. We're in the early stages."

"I understand. I'll just do my best," Dulcie replied. "I'll talk with you soon." She picked up her jacket and bag, and quickly left.

Nicholas Black had stood as she was leaving. He had been bred to stand when a lady entered or left the room, and it was now a mechanical instinct. He slowly sat again and took a deep breath, looking down at her cell phone. He had not told her the most critical piece of information. Along with the body of the woman, they had found a watertight tube. Rolled up in the tube was what appeared to be an incredibly valuable van Gogh painting which, he had just learned, had been stolen from a private collection the year before.

Dulcie was at the top of the suspect list.

Nick didn't like it.

*The aim of art is to represent not
the outward appearance of things,
but their inward significance.*
~ Aristotle

CHAPTER TWO

Dulcie walked slowly down the busy, hot street without seeing anything. Her mind was focused on the photograph of the dead woman. The sudden blast of a car horn made her look up and she realized she was at the waterfront, near the berth of her brother's boat. *'Maybe I'll see if he's around,'* she thought. *'He might be able to jar my memory.'*

Dan Chambers ran a relatively lucrative business taking tourists on rides around the bay. Several months earlier Dulcie had unexpectedly inherited a large sum of money. She had decided to become a silent partner with Dan in his business, and had invested in a moderately sized yacht that included a small but quite comfortable cabin where Dan now lived. Previously he had run the business from an old, ramshackle fishing boat while he lived in an apartment. He had played up the hokey coastal Mainer image for the business. This persona was gone now, however. Dan had discovered that having a higher end vessel not only allowed him to charge more per passenger, but also brought in more people who wanted a taste of what they believed was the good life. His best moneymakers were the champagne and caviar sunset cruises.

"If they only knew the reality," Dan would say as he looked around his small cabin. But then he would grin and think, *'I wouldn't trade it for the world!'*

Dulcie made her way down the wharf and saw a group of people walking toward her from the direction of Dan's boat. *'Just in,'* she thought, hoping it was his last run of the day. She wanted to simply float on the water for a while feeling the boat gently bob up and down as she turned over her thoughts. She saw Dan on the deck talking to his part-time first mate Freddie. "Hey, you guys know how to navigate this thing?" she yelled. The both looked up and laughed.

Freddie stepped over to the gangplank and held her arm carefully while she walked on board. *'Ever the gentleman,'* thought Dulcie. She smiled at him.

Freddie was a gem for sure although he had his quirks, as Dan was rapidly discovering. He had struck up a conversation with Freddie two months earlier on one of the bay tours. Freddie was retired and was looking for a part-time job. Or rather, his wife was looking for a part-time job for him. It seemed that she was on the verge of losing her mind with him at home and constantly underfoot. Dan always laughed when he remembered the conversation, because he thought Freddie's wife would even suggest that she could pay Freddie's wages. In the end, Freddie was hired and had learned quickly. Dan had found an excellent first mate at a very low hourly rate.

"You guys in for the day?" Dulcie asked.

"Ayuh," Freddy said wistfully. "Gotta take the wife to the Mall. She says she needs shoes." He looked at Dulcie thoughtfully, then down at her feet. Her black pumps were scuffed and had certainly seen better days. "No offense Miss, but how many pairs of shoes does a woman actually need?" he asked without looking up.

"Depends on the woman I suppose, Freddie," she replied, trying hard to sound serious. "In your case, I'd say the answer is always, 'One more'."

Freddie sighed. "That's what I was afraid of. Guess I'll see you tomorrow then?" he asked Dan.

"Yep. Nine work for you? We've got a tour at ten o'clock," said Dan.

Freddie nodded, turning around to straighten the rack of life vests that were already in perfect order. He gave them a final satisfied pat and continued onto the gangplank. "Afternoon, Miss" he said to Dulcie as he turned and stepped onto the dock.

"Bye Freddie! Good luck with the shoes!"

Reminded of his grim task ahead, Freddie walked back up the dock shaking his head slowly.

Dulcie turned to her brother. "Who is happier now that he's with you, Freddie or his wife?" she grinned.

Dan chuckled, "I'd say on any given day it's an even bet."

Dulcie looked around the deck. Every rope and line was perfectly coiled and in place. All of the striped seat cushions were positioned exactly the same distance apart. Even the little bags of potato chips in the snack basket for the passengers were perfectly ordered according to flavor with the labels facing in the same direction. Dulcie smiled. "He does keep things ship-shape, doesn't he? So different from your usual, let's call it *casual*, organization around here."

"Oh yes. Very ship-shape. Maybe that's one of the things sending the wife over the edge?"

Dulcie nodded. "If he does this at home it must drive her crazy! I wonder what she'll do this winter when he's not working?"

"Freddie says they just bought a place in Florida. That'll keep both of them occupied for a while. Plus, there are grandchildren down there too. Freddie's good with the kids so he'll keep busy." Dan looked back at Dulcie. "But, on a totally different subject, guess what I just got on email."

"I have absolutely no idea," Dulcie said, sinking into a seat cushion, marring its perfect alignment.

"An invitation to my high school reunion."

Dulcie made a gagging sound. "Tell me you aren't going," she said.

"Of course I'm going! I'm highly successful and," he puffed out his chest, "incredibly good looking! Why should I let all this go to waste if I can gloat about it?"

Dulcie smiled. Of course he would go. Dan was the easy-going fun guy in school that everyone liked. He could walk into any room and instantly start chatting regardless of whether he knew anyone or not. She had seen it hundreds of times. Dulcie did not have the same abilities. She had watched him carefully on many occasions, trying to learn how he did it but never could seem to adopt his calm, friendly manner completely.

Dulcie's job required her to attend many events, usually involving some sort of fundraising. Over the years she had learned to pretend that she actually was Dan during the first ten minutes when she felt the most uneasy, so that she could mimic his manner. She went straight home immediately after every event exhausted, whereas Dan would have been ready for the next venue on the evening's agenda. It was the one part of her job that she truly disliked.

"Well then, have fun. Give everyone my best." She yawned. Even the thought of it made her tired.

Dan just shook his head. They were so different. He changed the subject. "So what's new with you lately?"

She immediately sat up straight and swung her legs around off the seat to face him. "You'll never believe this. Remember the police guy, Detective Black?"

"The one who had a crush on you?" Dan grinned.

"Stop it, he did not. Okay, maybe he did. But nothing came of it. Anyway, I just saw him."

"You bumped into him?"

"Nope. He called me. And get this! He showed me a picture of a dead woman who washed up on the beach in Cape Elizabeth, *and* she had my cell phone number written on her hand!"

Dan's eyes widened. He sat down heavily on the seat beside her. "*What?*"

"Yup, you heard me. Nick... I mean Detective Black... stop laughing! He told me to call him Nick!" She swatted her brother. "He asked me if I knew her."

"Do you?"

"Well, it's strange. She looks familiar. I know I've seen her before, but I can't think where. She was in diving gear and her hair was wet which made it look dark so I couldn't really tell what color it was."

"You should call and ask him. Bet he'd know by now. Or they could get a blow-dryer at the morgue if it isn't quite dry yet." He smiled at his own ingenuity.

Dulcie stared at him. "I can't believe you just said that. But actually, I guess they probably would have hair dryers there." She shook her head vigorously in an attempt to remove the image of a hair dryer being used in the morgue, but wasn't successful. Her own dark hair began to spill out of the silver barrette that held it back. "I'm totally off subject here. The point is that I'm trying to figure out where I've seen her."

"You have about a billion events a year, so maybe one of those? I know that really narrows it down."

Dulcie looked rueful. "That and the fact that I see tons of people coming and going from the museum every day. Nope, I'll have to stew on this one."

"But what about your phone number on her hand? That's weird. Which hand was it?"

Dulcie's eyes narrowed as she glanced over at her brother. "Does it matter?"

"Well, it'd tell you if she's left handed or right handed."

"And how would that help me remember who she is?"

Dan tried to appear serious. It didn't work. He burst out laughing. "It's what they always do on those cop shows! You know, it turns into one of those critical pieces of information that totally solves the case and nobody thought of it until the very end when it's some kid who says it or the detective's wife who just makes an off-handed comment. I'll bet your Nicky Boy…"

"Detective Black to you, sir," she interjected.

"Oh, sorry, your *Detective Black* hasn't even thought of it yet!"

Dulcie rolled her eyes. "Dan, did you ever think that someone else might have written that number on her hand?"

He leaned back in his seat. "Oh yeah. I guess that could have happened."

Dulcie stood up and yawned again. "Well, I should get home. I've got a ton of stuff that I have to read which I really don't want to deal with, but I have no choice. Keep me posted on your exciting life?"

Dan smiled and nodded. "You too. I can barely keep up with you!"

She rolled her eyes again at him and climbed onto the gangplank, not an easy maneuver in a dress and high-heels.

If a man devotes himself to art,
much evil is avoided that
happens otherwise if one is idle.
~ Albrecht Durer

CHAPTER THREE

Lydia Davenport-Jones stepped out onto the front deck of her new home and smiled. The beach stretched out in front of her on both sides and the Atlantic was an endless body of blue marred only by the occasional foaming surf. Yes, this would certainly do for now, she thought.

Lydia's life had not always been quite so grand. Growing up inland, well inland, she had dreamed of the beach, the house on the ocean, the sailboat, and of course the handsome husband complete with docksiders and Ray-Bans. She had managed to acquire all of the above in a very short period of time.

And now she frowned. Was she truly happy? No. Despite the luxury surrounding her, she was not.

Clark Davenport-Jones was an idiot. She knew that. He carelessly spent the family money. His mother was furious with him perpetually. She disapproved of

Lydia, seeing her as a gold-digger. Maybe she was. But Lydia didn't really care about what Clark's mother thought. Lydia knew that she was much smarter, much more worthy, much more cautious then her husband. All that wealth was wasted on him. She sighed, staring out at the blue waves constantly rolling toward her.

Her plan was simple. Ignore the parents. The opinion of her in-laws really didn't matter in the end. Instead of trying to prove herself to them, she would take a much quicker route. She would get her hands on a large portion of money, invest it wisely, watch it grow as quickly as possible, then divorce Clark and his pretentious parents. The only difficult part had been the first bit. How could she siphon off money without anyone knowing about it?

A chance newspaper article provided the perfect solution. The art. Her mother-in-law was an avid collector, to the point where Lydia knew that she had forgotten about many of the pieces stuffed in their various houses. Why not simply slip some away, ever so slowly, and sell them? Who would know? And if they noticed them missing, they could have simply been lost in one of their many moves to a new property. That's what insurance was for after all, right?

Lydia had moved quickly. Her first piece was a 19th century miniature portrait. It wasn't really worth a huge amount, just a few thousand dollars. She had found a private collector in California and sold it to him under a false name. No one had even noticed. It was easy, and she had found it exciting compared with the endless boredom of life as Clark Davenport-Jones's wife.

Next she chose a sketch done by the fashion illustrator René Bouché. Again, nothing major, certainly not his best. She'd held her breath on that one. The buyer wanted authentication. She'd managed to find enough background information from the Internet to pacify him and had surreptitiously photocopied a file from her mother-in-law's desk that contained the work's provenance.

It had turned out to be surprisingly straightforward. No one knew except her sister, Jennifer. It had actually been Jennifer's idea originally - she had seen the article and shared it with Lydia. Lydia did the background work, while Jennifer was the front person. She was the older sister and always more daring than Lydia. Jennifer was also a bit of a black sheep; save for Lydia's wedding, her in-laws barely knew she existed. Or cared.

Lydia's frown deepened. She hadn't heard from Jennifer, and that was unusual. They typically communicated about the art by coded email. Jen would send a message to Lydia and ask her to meet somewhere. Usually this happened every three or four days. It had been a week now, and Lydia still hadn't heard anything. A chilly breeze blew over her and she shivered once, quickly. '*No*,' she thought. '*It's fine. Jen's just doing her thing, as always. The semi-lone wolf. She'll get in touch.*' But it was always Jen who emailed Lydia with their next meeting place, not the other way around. Jen insisted on that. She was very protective of her little sister.

'*I'll wait one more day*,' thought Lydia. '*That'll be a full week. Seven days. Then I'll send a quick text and see what's up.*' She nodded, as if to convince herself that all was well. Then she shivered once more and went inside.

CB

"Oh Clark, really! Why do you have to be so bothersome?" Alexia Kent rolled over on the bed, the sheet wrapping tightly around the sinuous curves of her body. "I mean, I know you just married her, but you don't have to go running back just yet. She's such an annoying little thing. Looks like a frightened puppy half the time. How long before you leave her?"

Clark Davenport-Jones was brushing his teeth. He spit into the sink and looked at Lexi in the mirror. She knew that look. She had just crossed the line.

"I think, my darling Lexi, that you and I need to take a little break for a while." He continued to stare at her reflection in the mirror until she cringed inwardly and looked away. Damn him. He always had the upper hand. Why did her parents have to be so damned old-money? What that really meant was, they had beautiful houses and antique furnishings, but no cash on hand. Who cared about having four houses if you couldn't buy Prada when you felt like it?

It wasn't like anyone came to visit them in their houses anyway. Lexi's parents were the most antisocial people she knew. They attended exactly three functions each year: the country club annual fundraising dinner-dance, the Christmas fête, and the party for her grandparent's anniversary. Otherwise, they were either on the golf course or on the boat. Or in one of the four houses.

Who were these people and how could they possibly be her parents? Lexi was nothing like them. She wanted to be at a party from the moment she woke until the very small hours of the morning when she finally fell into bed, which was usually not alone. She'd had an allowance from them for years, but it wasn't even close to what she needed. "You should get a job, Lexi," her father had said. Of course she could. She'd been sent off to the elite Dana Hall School, then to Brown University, so she certainly had the connections if not exactly the grades. She'd even made the attempt once, but when the offer came through they said she could only take off two weeks for vacation time. Two weeks? She had laughed out loud. That was ridiculous. The summer season was only getting started in two weeks. What would she do then, go back to work while everyone else had gin & tonics at the club? No, thank you.

Lexi smiled at Clark Davenport-Jones as he came out of the bathroom. She stood up and let the sheet cascade to the floor. "Clark, darling," she whispered, "You know you don't mean that. And if you do," she pouted, "You could at least leave me a little something so that I could buy myself a present until you can see me again? Something that you might like very much?"

Clark unriveted his eyes from her golden skin for long enough to reach for his wallet. He pulled out an American Express card and handed it to her. She giggled and kissed him, throwing her arms around his neck and pushing him back on the bed.

Clark left Lexi's Boston apartment an hour later wondering how his life had become so complicated. He thought he loved Lydia. She was so different. He had met her at the country club. She had been a waitress there and was always kind to him. No one was ever kind to him unless they wanted something, but she never seemed to want anything. Did she love him? He wasn't completely sure. She was so reserved. Certainly she had married him, but what did that ever have to do with love?

Lexi didn't love him; that was certain. She loved his money. And she loved having a good time, which included having him in her bed. It had to stop. He knew that. If he did truly love Lydia, it certainly had to stop. As he drove in the bright sunshine with the convertible top down to his new home in Maine on the tony Prouts Neck, he contemplated the various ways to end his relationship with Lexi. The easiest would be to terminate the credit card he'd just given her. Not only would she be embarrassed, she'd get the message immediately. The problem there, however, was that she would undoubtedly create a scene somewhere, somehow, and the truth would come out to Lydia that he hadn't been completely faithful to her, either while they were engaged or after they were married. No, he would have to talk with Lexi. And pay her off. He knew that ultimately it was the only way to permanently end the liaison.

Clark thought about Lydia. He would never have to pay off someone like her. She was so sweet, so pure. Why hadn't he ended it with Lexi earlier? The image of the sheet sliding down her body, the blonde hair curving over her shoulders flashed into his mind. Yes, he knew why. And he was a fool.

He steered the navy BMW into the drive of the new house. He instantly felt a wave of relief. It was their house. Not his parents', not Lexi's, not anyone's but his and Lydia's. He could relax. He could do what he wanted, say what he wanted. He and Lydia were so often of a like mind that many times he didn't even need to speak. She seemed to know what he was thinking before he did.

Lydia was incredibly smart. She should have gone on in school to become some sort of professor or lawyer or doctor but he knew that her family expectations had prevented that. It was odd how the people that she came from often said that they wanted someone to achieve, but felt threatened when it actually happened. They wanted Lydia to better herself and make something of her life certainly, but to truly move beyond what everyone else had become, to find great success, was unacceptable. They simply wouldn't allow it. When that happened you weren't a source of pride in family discussions, you were the one that was "too good" for everyone else. You were ostracized. Of course, Lydia had been ostracized anyway because she had committed the other mortal sin of "marrying up." That was even worse. It was the quick road to success and no one could stand for that. Clark felt sorry for her.

ॐ

Lydia looked out the window and saw the BMW pull into the driveway. She took a deep breath, steeling herself to play the part. Lydia knew that Clark believed she was so shy, so innocent. In some ways, she was certainly. In other ways, she had no problem taking advantage. She knew what it was like to go without, to never have enough.

She also knew about Lexi. Clark didn't realize this, but Lydia was no fool. She had seen the two of them at her engagement party and even at her wedding reception. Clark had explained that Lexi was a former girlfriend. "From a lifetime ago," he had said, but Lydia knew he was still living that life. She hated him for it. But she had to pretend, at least for a while longer.

Lydia was half way to her goal of a quarter of a million dollars. It wasn't a fortune, certainly, but it was enough to buy her a decent place to live and to get started on a new career. Plus, she knew that if she got greedy, people would begin to suspect. *'Keep it small,'* she thought. *'Get just enough for what you need, then you can move on.'* Yes, it was enough.

Life is the art of drawing
without an eraser.
~ John W. Gardner

CHAPTER FOUR

"Ross, you can't be serious!" Amelia Davenport-Jones stared at her husband. "You know she only married him for his money!"

Ross looked away wondering, not for the first time, what he had ever seen in her. He slowly turned back, "Not unlike yourself?"

He didn't see it coming. She slapped him full on the cheek. Years of swinging a golf club had given her an impressive amount of muscle even if she was over sixty. He glared at her, then went into the kitchen, rummaged through the freezer, and pulled out a bag of peas which he held to his face. He supposed he had deserved it, almost. Her family had nearly as much as his, but he had added nicely to the sum as an equine vet specializing in thoroughbreds. He'd made an excellent career for himself with the horses and, better yet, it had given him excuses to stay away from his wife with increasing regularity.

Ross liked Lydia. Maybe she had married Clark for his money, but did that matter? If they were happy and got along well, that was the only point. Lydia seemed supportive and so smart. And maybe she'd make something of him, which was more than Ross and Amelia had been able to do with their son. Ross wanted to promote that as much as he could. He had tried to get Clark interested in his work with the horses. For one summer, when Clark was about sixteen years old, Ross had brought him along on nearly all of his calls. But by August, Ross learned that his son had not used his newfound knowledge for any sort of career, but instead to bet on the horses. Which he still managed to do poorly.

Ross shook his head slightly, a difficult maneuver while holding a bag of peas to the side of it. Clark took after his mother and that was all. Ross found himself taking more pride in the horses than in his own son. He wondered if that was really so unusual.

Amelia ran her hand under the cold tap water in the bathroom. She really shouldn't have slapped him like that. They were never physical with each other. In that way or any other, for that matter. She couldn't remember the last time they had been even remotely close to intimate. Maybe he had taken a lover? She snorted at the thought.

Turning off the tap she dried her hand, then went into the bedroom to change. Today she was planning to have lunch with the director of the Maine Museum of Art, Dr. Chambers. She had read that Dulcinea

Chambers had inherited a large sum of money from the former board chairman who had been killed recently in a very hushed-up situation. Of course Amelia knew all of the details, but she kept that to herself. What she wanted to know now was whether the museum was interested in selling a certain work to the Davenport-Jones collection. Her lust for buying art was nearly insatiable, which was why she hoped that a quick, quiet sale would keep the price low. She pulled out a seersucker skirt from her closet and tugged it on.

 G8

Dulcie was not looking forward to lunch. She found herself having a love-hate relationship with her job. Most of it was love, but this aspect, dealing with people like Amelia Davenport-Jones, certainly was not. "Why don't these people just send a check and be done with it?" she said out loud. "Why do they always want to have lunch?"

Rachel giggled. Dulcie glanced up quickly. She hadn't noticed her assistant standing in the doorway. "Excited about eating out today?" she grinned. Dulcie let out a low groan. "You could always pretend to be sick. I could call her and beg off for you," Rachel suggested.

"No, no. Thank you, but no. I have to get it over with. Rachel, it's the schmoozing that I hate, not the eating. Although why is it always at some posh place, or worse yet *The Club* as they always say? Why can't we just go to the Jade Palace and have the blue-flaming pu-pu platter?"

Rachel burst out laughing. "Can you imagine Amelia Davenport-Jones eating mystery meat on a stick? I'd actually pay good money to see that!"

"Thanks Rachel. I'll savor that image in my head today to keep my spirits up. Do you need me for something?"

Rachel shook her head, her brown curls springing out from her attempt to contain them in a bright green headband. "Not really. Just wondered what your schedule was. Want me to call you a cab for the lunch date?"

Dulcie shook her head. "I think I'd rather walk, even if it is hot out. We're meeting just beyond Dan's boat and I want to talk to him if he's around."

Rachel nodded and disappeared. Dulcie followed her out of the office door and wandered the main gallery for a few moments. The museum was cool and quiet. Although they always needed the income from ticket sales, Dulcie was happy when the museum had few visitors. She stood in front of her favorite work, a watercolor of Winslow Homer's done in Bermuda. She was always amazed by the color and simplicity. It made her feel calm and happy.

"Dr. Chambers?"

Dulcie jumped and whirled around. A hand on her arm steadied her. "I'm sorry! I didn't mean to startle you." Detective Nicholas Black held her arm for a brief moment longer than necessary, then let go. "I just wanted to return your phone." He was taller than Dulcie remembered. Or maybe it was just that she was wearing flats today rather than her typical mid-height heels.

"Oh! Thank you!" Dulcie found herself slightly breathless. "That's nice of you. And thanks for being so quick with it. Did you find anything useful?"

Was she poking fun at him? Nick couldn't tell. "No, we didn't. And I didn't really expect that we would. But my supervisor would have been all over me if I hadn't followed procedure."

"I understand completely," said Dulcie. "Are there any leads though? I'm still trying to remember how I know that woman. I have seen her before, I just can't think where."

"It'll come to you, I'm sure." He shifted back and forth nervously for a moment, then said, "Would you like to go have lunch and talk about the case a little? It might jog your memory."

Dulcie laughed. "You have no idea how much I'd love to, but unfortunately I'm *following procedure* as well today. I'm meeting a potential donor for lunch. Amelia Davenport-Jones. Do you know of her?"

Of course Nick knew of her, but he could not tell Dulcie. Not yet. His parents and the Davenport-Joneses had been friends in Boston. They still were. But he didn't have anything to do with them now. He had been effectively cut off since turning his back on a lucrative career in law, and instead choosing a life of detective work. His family could not forgive him for taking on what they considered to be such a low occupation and not following tradition in the family firm. "Yes, I've heard of her," he replied.

"I'm not sure who hasn't!" said Dulcie. "This is one of the least enjoyable parts of my job. Fundraising, that is. But it's necessary. I have to put up with it and play the game."

"I know that well," said Nick. He'd forgotten how shiny her dark hair was, especially under the soft museum lights.

"I'm going to try to get together with my brother later this afternoon on his boat. I'm hoping to catch him on my way to lunch and see if he's free. He's good at jarring my memory. Want to meet us there?"

Yes, a third party would be a good idea, thought Nick. "That's perfect. Can you give me a call with the time?" He nodded toward her phone, now in her hand.

"Yes, I will. And now I have to go. Hopefully, I'll see you later!" She smiled and left the gallery.

Nick stood frozen for a moment. "Hopefully," he breathed to himself.

I invent nothing.
I rediscover.
~ Auguste Rodin

CHAPTER FIVE

Nick slid his legs under the safety rope along the edge of the yacht and dangled his feet over the clear water. He could see a crab scuttling along below him, and the seaweed swayed gently back and forth in the light waves. *'Good thing I'm wearing lace-up shoes,'* he thought. *'I'd lose anything else in the drink for sure.'*

"Beer?" asked Dan behind him.

"Yes, please!" Nick reached back and took the bottle that Dan held out. He jerked the cap off and swigged with one quick motion. The icy cold beer bubbled down his throat. He wiped his mouth and grinned at Dan. "Thanks. Needed it."

Dan sat on the edge of the boat beside him with his own bottle. "Tough case?"

"Yep. I'm stumped. I really wish Dulcie could remember who that woman is. We're coming up empty. Nothing on dental records so far. DNA testing is taking forever. No one in the local dive shops knows anybody that's been in recently who seems to fit her description."

"Well, that's what Dulcie wants to do right now. Dredge through the memory banks with me. That is, if she ever gets here." He looked up the dock behind them just to see her rounding the corner. "Ah, and speak of the devil."

Nick spun around quickly. Dan smiled to himself. *'Yup,'* he thought. *'He's still interested.'*

Dulcie waved. *'They're getting on well,'* she thought, seeing them chatting over beer. As she climbed on board she looked at them both with mock awe. "What, no one will jump up and immediately assist a lady with a cold one?"

Nick had already begun to get up but Dan stopped him. Dan cleared his throat. "First of all, Nick is a guest so he wouldn't have to. Secondly, you're my sister and you know where the fridge is." He held up his bottle in a mock toast. Dulcie flipped her hair over her shoulder, feigning annoyance.

When she came back she sat down with them, beside Nick. She tried to twist the cap off the bottle but it wouldn't budge. "Could you please get this for me, Officer?" She batted her eyelashes.

Dan snorted. "On so many levels that's just bad, Dulcie. You see, he's a Detective, not an Officer. Also, I've never seen you *not* get a beer cap off, and finally… well, I can't even think of anything else right now but I'm sure I'll come up with something. Oh, I know! You're horrible at flirting!"

Dulcie ignored him and accepted the open bottle back with a smile. "Thank you, sir," she said to Nick. *'And that was fun!'* she thought to herself.

"So, have you come up with any ideas?" said Nick. "Any vague memories?"

"Not really. I know I've seen her. But I also know that it hasn't been recently. She's from a long while ago I think. I just wish I could place her. The problem is, I've been too busy lately and I can't let my mind just drift. I think that's the only way I'll figure it out."

"What have you been working on?" asked Dan.

"Lots of fundraising. Which I loathe, as you know. Too much schmoozing. For once I'd like to just sit down with someone who's completely loaded and talk intelligently about art. Instead it's a who's who of the turnout at the last fundraiser or the caterers for the next. Although today, I did have kind of a different meeting."

"How so?" asked Nick.

"Well, you said that you know of the Davenport-Jones family? They summer up here. They've been collectors for quite a while. Amelia Davenport-Jones got in touch last week and asked me to lunch. I thought it would be the usual, but turns out she's interested in buying something from the museum."

"That seems strange. Would you sell anything?" asked Dan.

"Ordinarily, no, but she's done her homework. We did put a piece on auction about a year ago but then withdrew it the day before. The board had second thoughts. But with the museum's heating system needing upgrades now before the winter, they might reconsider for the right price. Nothing glamorous about raising cash for building maintenance, so no cocktail parties. I have to say, selling something is my favorite kind of fundraising. It lets us cull the collection, which is healthy, brings in cash, and there's no schmoozing involved. Everybody is happy. Especially me!" She smiled.

Dan was quiet for a few moments, looking into the water. "I know that name." He thought for another minute. "Hey, didn't Lydia Hully marry Clark Davenport-Jones recently? Remember her? I just saw her name on the class list for the reunion."

"I have no idea, but if you say so." She looked at Nick. "Dan's the extrovert of the family. He keeps up with that stuff. I should pay more attention probably, but I'm just not very interested. I figure that if I haven't stayed in touch all along, what could I have in common with them now?"

"Well, in this case, maybe a wealthy donor?" Dan smirked.

"Good point." Dulcie sipped her beer. "Good point," she said again quietly. Something was stirring in her mind. She could feel it. She got up, walked to the bow of the boat, and then sat down again, alone.

Nick glanced at her, then at Dan. "She all right?" he asked quietly.

"She does that. Something hits her and she goes away until she works it out. When she was a kid people thought she was rude. She learned to be more polite, which she wasn't just now since she's here with me. Sorry about that."

"No, it's ok. I know she has a huge job. I appreciate that she's even giving me the time to talk about things." They both looked out across the harbor, watching a pleasure craft attempt to navigate a tight docking procedure. It bumped nearly every boat around it. They both laughed.

"Hey!" Both men jumped as Dulcie yelled from the bow. "I've got it!" She clamored back to them. "Dan, that's it! Remember Lydia Hully had an older sister? I think her name was Jennifer? She and Lydia looked a lot alike. I think the woman in the picture, the one that died, might have been Jennifer Hully!"

"Dang, girl." Dan pulled his legs up from over the side. "Hang on one second..." He scooted into the cabin, and came out a moment letter pulling a wad of papers from a thick envelope. "The reunion committee sent some pictures." He leafed through the papers, then stopped. "There's Lydia. Does she look familiar?"

Nick and Dulcie nearly clocked heads leaning over the photo. "Wow, that does look like her!" said Nick.

"Sure does," replied Dulcie. "Now I'm wondering which one it actually might be."

Nick reached for his phone and began scrolling through the photos to find the images of the dead woman on the beach again.

"I know how to find out for sure," said Dan. He pulled out his own cell phone.

"Who are you calling?" asked Nick.

"The reunion committee chair. They may have heard from Lydia recent..." Dan put up his hand to stop anyone from speaking, and said, "Hey Jack! Dan Chambers! Great to hear from you! ... Yeah, I'm definitely coming! Wouldn't miss it! But hey, quick question. Have you heard form Lydia Hully? Did she get in touch? ... Today? ...Oh, too bad. I'd like to have seen her. OK, just wondering. I'll talk to you soon before the big event. Thanks!" He put the phone back in his pocket. "Lydia called them today and said she couldn't make it."

"So she's still alive! Then it might be Jennifer. And I wonder if Lydia has seen her recently," Nick said. "How close were they?"

"Don't know," replied Dan. "I remember seeing Jennifer around, back when we were in school, so they must have been fairly close. I think she was only a couple years older."

"Yes, you're right." Dulcie had been silent, thinking. "If I remember correctly, Jennifer was kind of a daredevil. I think she had a motorcycle for a while that she rode to high school. The boys couldn't get over it."

Nick shook his head, smiling. "I can imagine!"

A heavy mist had been creeping slowly across the bay toward them. Dulcie drained her beer and shivered. She turned to Nick. "Well, that mystery may be solved, but we still don't know why she would be calling me. I haven't seen her in years, and I don't know how she could have my cell number, although it's far from private. Do you need me anymore right now? I really have to get home and get some things done." She handed her empty bottle to Dan.

Nick shook his head. "No, but if you think of any reason why..."

"Yes, you'll be the first to know!" Dulcie smiled at him, gave her brother a punch on the arm, and jumped off the boat onto the dock. Half way back toward to the street she pulled out her cell phone.

"Who do you think she's calling?" asked Nick. His eyes hadn't left her.

Dan chuckled. "Jade Palace. Chicken fried rice. And steamed vegetables if she's feeling fat, beef teriyaki and an egg roll if she isn't. She has them on speed dial."

*I would rather die of passion
than of boredom.*
~ Vincent van Gogh

CHAPTER SIX

Ross Davenport-Jones had been driving aimlessly, or so he thought. Before he realized it, he was approaching Winterhaven Stables. His only true love was there, a chestnut mare named Attagirl. She was a thoroughbred, recently retired. Her career had been moderately successful, to the point where her owner, Donald Winters, thought she could breed more success if sired appropriately. But Ross knew that Winters didn't love her the way he did. As always, Donald Winters was in it for the cash.

Winters took care of his horses well, certainly. He spared few expenses in stabling them, kept them safe and healthy for racing, and looked after them when their running careers were over. You couldn't fault him for doing the right thing when it came to his horses. They were his indulgence. Yet they were only an indulgence to the point where they were still income generating. Ross doubted if Donald would continue in the business if it did not provide a positive cash flow.

Ross viewed it differently. Horses were in his blood. His father had been a trainer and had made a fortune from his work along with some very successful long-shot bets. He had introduced Ross to the racing world at an early age. Ross loved the smell of the stables, the sound of the hooves beating on the dirt, and the feel of a well-cared-for horse's coat after he'd brushed it. He remembered that feeling even as a young child. His father had taught him to respect the horses, "And they'll respect you, too," he had said. He was right.

His father had been a gentle man. Ross learned from him that every horse had a personality. Once you knew the horse well, understood their likes, dislikes, and motivations, everything was easy. As always, his father had been completely correct.

Attagirl had the kind of personality that owners dreamed of. She was easygoing and hard-working, in the paddock and on the training course. When she was at the starting gate, however, it was as though she was a different creature. Her eyes would light up. Once, Ross swore he saw her mane stand on end. A demon would emerge that would not subside until she crossed the finish line, often ahead of everyone else. Sometimes Ross thought that she didn't actually need a jockey.

Although her racing days were over, Ross wanted her. He wanted to own her. He wanted to continue to see her run, to see what foals she could produce, to be a part of her life and make her a part of his.

Everyone had a price, even Donald Winters. And Ross had the inside track with a plan that he thought would be perfect. He knew that he probably couldn't afford the horse outright. Well, he could actually, but Amelia would kill him. Plus, there were the increasing expenses of Clark's, now that he was married but still unemployed. The trust fund seemed to have run dry for him all too quickly. Ross knew that if he wanted Attagirl at a reasonable price, he would need to lay the groundwork quietly and cleverly. First, he had to convince Donald that she wasn't quite as healthy as he thought. That would make him consider selling. Then, Ross needed to offer enough cash for her to make the sale go through quickly.

Convincing Donald of the first part was not going to be easy. He knew his horses, and anything obvious would cost Ross the lucrative Winterhaven Stables as a client, not to mention ruin his reputation on the circuit. If Attagirl suddenly became ill, Ross bought her for a discounted price, then she was miraculously better, he'd be in the midst of a lawsuit for sure. That's when he realized that he needed an intermediary in his plan.

Jennifer Hully had been the perfect choice. He had met the sister of his new daughter-in-law at Clark's wedding. She had an aura about her that terrified most men: beautiful, confident, and fearless. But best of all, it was obvious to Ross that Jennifer couldn't stand his wife Amelia.

Ross and Jennifer had struck up a relationship that could not entirely be called a friendship. They shared mutual interests certainly. The first time they had lunch together was merely by chance at a local clam shack. He had bumped into her the day after the wedding, and it seemed rude not to join her at the outdoor picnic table for twenty minutes while she was finishing her lunch.

He had been surprised by her knowledge of horse racing. "I like betting," she said. "It's different from gambling. Gambling is all about numbers and probabilities and bluffing. Betting on horses requires knowledge. You have to understand animals, people, weather, track records… and just plain luck." He had asked her if she ever wanted to own a horse. She hesitated, thinking for a moment, then shook her head. "Too much work, and I don't want to put my eggs in one basket. I'd rather learn about all of the baskets and all of the eggs, then just put my money on the ones I think are best." He had known then that she would do quite well for his plan.

It was natural for Jennifer to want to spend time with him. His knowledge of horses was seemingly bottomless. But he was always careful to keep their liaisons away from anyone else in the racing realm. That would interfere with his plan. No one could suspect that he and Jennifer knew each other so well.

He introduced his plan to her about two months after that first lunch. He felt that he could trust her sufficiently by then. It was simple. He would sicken Attagirl just slightly, but enough so that Donald Winters would not want to keep her. Then Jennifer would approach Winters with an interest in buying the mare. She would offer him a cash sum, all of which would be fronted by Ross. Then Jennifer would be compensated well for her work in the transaction, and Attagirl's ownership would be signed over to Ross after a reasonable period of time.

As he drove, Ross turned over the plan again in his mind for the hundredth time. He steered his old Land Rover onto the dirt road of Winterhaven Stables, slowly drove by the training track, and eased to a stop by the paddock. He leaned his head back on the seat's headrest and closed his eyes for several seconds before taking a deep breath, opening the door, and sliding out of the vehicle with his medical bag in hand.

ೞ

Dulcie had been drinking coffee that was by now at room temperature. She took one more gulp, made a face, and swallowed hard. She sat in her office looking blankly out the window at the fishing boats. Jennifer Hully. Why on earth would Jennifer Hully want to be in touch with her? Strange.

And stranger still was the fact that Lydia had recently married Amelia Davenport-Jones's son. Amelia hadn't mentioned it, but then why would she? She wouldn't have any idea that Dulcie knew Lydia, although "knew" was probably a bit of a stretch. They had merely gone to school together years before.

Dulcie smirked. "She did well, though, to marry into that family," she said aloud. Dulcie herself wasn't without money now, although the loss of a good friend and mentor was the price that was paid. Joshua Harriman, the museum's chief benefactor and chairman of the board had left her a million dollars in his will after he had been killed tragically. She still felt sick thinking about it. Dulcie shook her head to clear away the shadows.

How could she find out more about Jennifer Hully? Would Nick have contacted Lydia by now to tell her that her sister had died? Probably, so it wouldn't be appropriate to call her and chat about Jennifer. But maybe Nick could arrange a meeting with the three of them? She decided to call him.

The phone rang only once when she heard his voice. "Dulcie?"

Dulcie thought, *'I guess I shouldn't be surprised that he has me programmed into his phone since this is our second case together.'* That idea seemed odd to her. She'd never imagined herself as any sort of crime-solving entity before. "Hi Nick. How are you?" she quickly answered.

"Good. What's up?" He grimaced thinking that he hadn't been exactly polite. He could have at least asked how she was, or even thanked her for identifying the woman on the beach. He took a deep, silent breath.

She didn't seem to notice, however. "I've been thinking about Jennifer Hully and why she would have my number written on her hand. Have you been in touch with Lydia yet to tell her about her sister?"

It was the worst part of his job. He hated it. He tried to get his partner, Adam Johnson to do it for him whenever he could but Adam usually just shook his head with a sad smile and said, "Ayuh, nice try. Not gonna happen. I've done my share."

Nick sighed. "No, not yet. But I'm going over to her house this afternoon. I spoke with her husband. He told me that she would be around then, and I need to see her in person for this. I have to see her reaction. Why did you want to know? Do you have a question that you want me to ask her?"

Dulcie hesitated. She did not really have a question other than, "Why did your sister have my cell phone number written on her hand when she died?" She thought for a moment. "Well Nick, other than the obvious question about my phone number, I just wanted to talk with her a little about her sister. I wanted to see if there was some connection I could establish. This doesn't make a lot of sense."

"Nope, they never do at this point. Do you want to come with me? It may not be pretty, but it could be the best time to find out a few things. People tend to talk in a strangely intimate way when they get news like this." He held his breath. On the one hand, he wanted her to come. She had a way of seeing everything very clearly, and certainly differently than he would. On the other hand, he did not want to subject her to a scene. They did need any scrap of information that they could possibly get, though. Yes, she should come. He heard her voice distantly.

"Nick? Can you hear me? Are you still there?"

"Oh, sorry. I was distracted. What was that?"

"I said that I'd like to come if you think it's all right. I won't say anything until you give me the go-ahead. If she recognizes me, she'll think it's strange that I'm there."

"Yes, we'll explain that as quickly as we can."

"Good. Shall I meet you there or do you want to go together?"

"We should go together. Can I pick you up at one-thirty? Her house is out on Prouts Neck. We'll easily get there by two o'clock."

"Yes, that sounds fine," said Dulcie. "I'll be at the museum. Just come around to the front entrance. I'll be outside there watching for you."

"Perfect. See you then," he said. The call clicked off.

Dulcie leaned back in her chair and looked at the dregs of her coffee. She glanced at the clock. Noon. *'Guess I'd better get some lunch if I'm going to be ready by one-thirty. This won't be easy,'* she thought. She stood up, grabbed her purse and headed for the door.

ভ

At precisely five minutes before two o'clock Nick steered his car into the gravel drive of Clark and Lydia Davenport-Jones's home. The house itself was a modest bungalow-style cottage with a large porch on the front. The view was anything but modest. Situated just above the sand dunes, it looked over a wide expanse of honey-colored beach and the glistening Atlantic Ocean. Without realizing what she was doing, Dulcie exhaled a long, low whistle.

Nick laughed softly. "Yeah, doesn't hurt to marry money, does it?" His own mind raced back to the summer beach house that his family kept in Chatham out on Cape Cod. He had known this life very, very well. And rejected it.

They got out of the car and rang the bell. A man in madras shorts, a faded polo shirt, and docksiders answered. Nick showed his badge, identifying himself and shook his hand. "Yes, we spoke on the phone. I'm Clark Davenport-Jones. I'm sure this isn't good news, is it."

Nick shook his head. "If we could see your wife, please."

Clark looked inquisitively at Dulcie, but then gestured them in. "Lydia's in the kitchen." He ushered them through. The kitchen was at the front of the house and had windows looking out toward the beach. Pearly quartz countertops gleamed in the sunshine. The room opened directly onto a spacious sitting area with furniture all slipcovered in white. Gentle, detailed paintings of shells hung on the walls. Throw pillows, perfectly placed, were white as well but with textured patterns and fabrics. French doors led to the generous front porch that wrapped around the house.

Nick introduced himself and Dulcie. Lydia looked at her oddly, as if vaguely recognizing her. Nick gestured to the porch and suggested that they sit outside. Lydia had not yet spoken.

Comfortably seated on the designer wicker furniture, Nick turned to Lydia. He cleared his through. "I'm afraid that I have some very bad news for you, Mrs. Davenport-Jones."

"Please, just call me Lydia." Her voice was very small.

"Lydia. I'm sorry to tell you that we believe your sister Jennifer has died. We'll of course need someone to identify her. That could be you or another close family member if you're not up to it."

Lydia sat very still. Dulcie wasn't even sure that she was breathing. Then, in a faint whisper, she said, "I knew something was wrong. I knew it. I knew it." She began rocking back and forth convulsively but her face did not change. Clark slid over on the settee beside her and put an arm around her. Her face was still frozen as she rocked back and forth with such force that she moved him along with her.

Without warning, she stopped. "How?" she said, looking at Nick. The single word came out as a sort of strangled cough. Dulcie thought that Lydia had stopped breathing again.

"I'm afraid she drowned in a scuba diving accident. She was found on a beach in Cape Elizabeth two days ago. It's taken us this long to learn who she was. She had no identification on her."

Lydia inhaled loudly. One huge gulp of air. She looked at Dulcie but couldn't seem to speak.

Nick followed her gaze. "This is Dr. Chambers from the Maine Museum of Art. She helped identify your sister. All of you went to high school together years ago, evidently."

The thought of high school took Lydia's mind out of the present. Dulcie watched as she relaxed, her body sinking down into the cushions. A bit of color came back into her face. "I knew you looked familiar," she said softly.

Dulcie leaned forward and put her hand on Lydia's knee. "I remember your sister was always a brave soul, more so than I could ever be. Didn't she ride a motorcycle, even in high school?"

A slight smile came across Lydia's face. "Yes," she murmured. "Jennifer was the daring one. She always wanted to go faster, to win every race, try out new things." Her eyes welled. "She pushed everything, for sure, but she wasn't stupid. She never ignored safety. She always wore a helmet and boots on the motorcycle. And I know she would never have gone diving alone. She talked about that once. She knew other divers, so she could always find someone to go with her." Lydia stared out over the ocean. "Why wouldn't anyone have known she was missing?" she said, as though to herself instead of to the others sitting with her.

Nick watched her carefully. He had learned to read the signs. He knew when people were faking their sorrow. He knew what real pain looked like. This was real. This was pain. Yet there was something else. Her immediate reaction had been one of shock, but it was almost as though she had been prepared for it, fearing the worst. Could that have been because she was perpetually worried about her sister, who liked to test the limits, or did Lydia know of something her sister was doing that was more specific?

Dulcie said, "Lydia, Detective Black brought me into all of this because of something odd. Your sister had my phone number written on her hand. I really didn't know her well years ago, and certainly haven't spoken to her since high school. Do you know why she might have wanted to get in touch with me?"

Lydia flinched. The art. Had Jennifer planned to say something to Dulcie? Why would she call her? Had she called her? No, she couldn't have, or Dulcie wouldn't be asking in the first place.

"I'm sorry. I... I don't know why she would have your number. She never mentioned you. I don't think she knows a lot about art. Or knew a lot, I mean...." Lydia began to cry in earnest. She buried her head in Clark's chest. He wrapped a protective arm around her.

"Can we do this later?" he asked Nick.

"Yes, but please let's try as soon as possible. At this point I'd suggest getting in touch with her doctor," he nodded toward Lydia "in case she needs to speak with a counselor." He pulled his card out of his pocket and handed it to Clark. "Give me a call if either of you think of anything. Day or night. I'll get in touch with you again tomorrow to see if we can follow up on this. We also need to have positive identification."

Clark nodded. He slowly rocked Lydia back and forth.

Dulcie smiled at him in what she hoped was a comforting way, then stood with Nick. They both left quietly. Nick held the car door open for Dulcie then eased it shut as quietly as possible. He walked around the back slowly and heaved a huge sigh as he slid behind the wheel. "I hate doing that," he said, leaning his head back and briefly closing his eyes.

She nodded. "It has to be awful, every time. But you're very good at it. You're good at making people feel at ease."

Nick lifted his head and glanced at her. "I try. It helps in my line of work to make people feel at ease. They open up sooner." He started the engine and backed out of the driveway. They drove slowly through the winding roads that crisscrossed between extremely well kept homes with manicured grounds. At last they reached the main road.

"Want to get something to eat?" asked Dulcie. "I have some thoughts."

Nick tightened his grip on the steering wheel. '*Not a date, not a date*,' he told himself so firmly that he thought he had actually said it out loud. "Yeah, sure. Good idea," he heard himself saying. Dulcie pointed to a sign ahead on the road, and Nick pulled into a small restaurant that served nearly every kind of fried seafood imaginable.

At mid-afternoon, no one was in the dining room. They went to a table by a window and sat. There were still crumbs strewn in front of them from the previous occupants. Eventually an expressionless teenage girl came out with a wet rag and wiped off the table. She threw the soggy mess on the next table over, pulled a battered note pad from her back pocket and said, "Whaddya want?"

Dulcie looked at Nick and nearly laughed. She had grown up with places like this. He looked a bit like a fish out of water. "How 'bout we split some fried scallops, fried clams, and French fries?"

Nick nodded. "Sounds good to me."

The waitress scribbled and, without looking up said, "Drink?"

Dulcie ordered an iced tea. Nick asked for a sparkling water. The waitress peered at him from beneath shaggy eyebrows and, without lifting her head, said, "We only got Poland Spring. Think that'll cover it?"

"Um, yes. That's fine. Thank you," he mumbled.

Dulcie stared hard at the table to force herself not to laugh. The waitress left and, regaining her composure, Dulcie looked back up at Nick. "You know what I thought was strange?"

"The fact that our waitress leaves the cleaning rag right out in the dining room?"

Dulcie laughed. "Maybe it's a bus-your-own-table kind of place."

"I'm not sure what kind of place it is. Maybe we should cancel our order...."

"No, don't be silly. These places are all up and down the coast. They're fine. Besides, nothing can survive deep-frying so the only thing that really can kill you is the fat itself. And that takes years."

Nick smiled. Dulcie worked in such a glamorous, rarified world, yet she was so down to earth. Genuine. Real. Very much unlike the women he had always been with in the past. Not that there were many.

The waitress brought in their drinks. She handed Nick the bottled water without a glass and sauntered back into the kitchen. The bottle was barely cold. He looked at Dulcie and they burst out laughing.

"OK, so tell me what you thought was strange," he said as he unscrewed the lid and tentatively took a sip.

Yes, back to work, Dulcie thought. "Here's the odd thing," she said. "Remember that I put my hand on Lydia's knee? I noticed that when I mentioned my phone number, she was startled. She flinched. I felt her jump, just slightly. Why would she do that? She was distraught over her sister dying under those circumstances, for sure. She was adamant over the fact that Jennifer wouldn't be diving alone. Any of those things would clearly upset her. But why would my phone number startle her? What bothered her about Jennifer contacting me?"

"Good point. That is strange. Any ideas?"

"Nope, not one. But the other thing that seems too coincidental is that I just met with Lydia's mother-in-law."

Nick sat back and stared at her. It was all spinning. Spinning quickly. In his work, coincidences were practically nonexistent. There was always a connection, a reason that explained it all. But finding the connection often seemed impossible.

Lydia flinched when Dulcie mentioned that Jennifer was going to call her. Dulcie had just spoken with Lydia's mother-in-law Amelia. Jennifer was already dead when Dulcie had met with Amelia. Dulcie was the common thread. But why?

"Jennifer would have been dead when you had lunch with Amelia. Do you think Amelia could have known?" asked Nick.

"Or cared?" said Dulcie. Then she shook her head. "No, she's a cold fish, definitely, but I can't imagine she's that cold. She would have mentioned something about a death in the family, I would think."

Nick wasn't quite so sure. He knew that Amelia Davenport-Jones would never think of Jennifer, or even Lydia for that matter, as family. He decided to put it in the back of his mind for the moment and let it simmer.

The waitress reappeared with enormous baskets of unidentifiable fried items. She slid them on the table along with a big bottle of ketchup. "Lemme know if you need anything else," she said and without waiting for them to reply, she left.

Nick looked at Dulcie. "I suppose asking for cocktail sauce is out of the question?"

Inspiration does exist
but it must find you working.
~ Pablo Picasso

CHAPTER SEVEN

After Nick dropped Dulcie off at her townhouse, he decided to check back in at the station. He strode into the communal office space and grabbed some coffee from the pot in the corner, hoping that it was reasonably fresh. He walked back to his desk blowing on it and nearly tripped over Johnson's foot. His partner was sitting in Nick's chair. Nick slopped coffee on his hand and, quickly putting the cup down, flapped his fingers in the air. "Ow, ow, hot, ow!" He looked up at Johnson through narrowed eyes. "What the hell are you doing at my desk?"

Johnson slowly smiled. "Well, first of all, watching the performance." Nick stopped flapping and sat down on the edge of the desk, wiping his hand off on his pant-leg. "But secondly, I'm wondering if you've seen this." He slid a manila envelope toward Nick. "Coroner's report," he said, nodding toward it.

Nick slid his wet coffee cup out of the way and picked up the folder. Flipping through it absently he said, "Let me guess. She drowned."

"Well yes, of course she drowned."

"Because she ran out of air."

"Yeesss, she ran out of air. So she drowned. Right on so far. That why you went to them 'spensive schools?"

Nick sighed. "Johnson, I was a young man when this conversation started."

"Well then, read the damned report!" He leaned forward. "Here's the juicy bit." He pointed with a chubby finger half way down the page:

Ketamine found in victim's saliva. Recommend further testing of diving equipment and clothing.

Nick looked up at his partner. "What's ketamine?"

"Well, I took the liberty of looking it up." He jerked his head toward the computer on Nick's desk.

Nick gasped theatrically. "You mean you used the computer?"

"That I did. Stop mocking me. You'd have been proud. And here's what I found," he cleared his throat and read aloud, "Ketamine: a dissociative anesthetic used in the treatment of animals and humans." Johnson looked up at his partner and continued, "So, being the brilliant researcher that I am..."

"And you are," Nick added.

Johnson peered over his reading glasses at Nick. "Yes, I certainly am. So, being brilliant and all, I looked up 'dissociative anesthetic.' Know what that is, smarty pants?"

"Enlighten me."

Johnson cleared his throat again. "It's a hallucinogen. It blocks signals from the conscious mind. Users can be in a state of sensory deprivation or even in a trance." He took off his reading glasses, tossed them on the desk, leaned back and folded his arms.

"Huh!" said Nick. "Well that certainly puts a spin on things!"

"Yep, certainly does!"

"She had a reputation as a daredevil, but I doubt she would have been stupid enough to take a hallucinatory drug, then go diving."

"Right. So somebody slipped it to her."

"Have we tested her equipment for anything? Was her mouthpiece tested?"

"Not yet, but I've ordered tests already. Figured if it wasn't there, no harm done. But if we find traces, we'll have narrowed things down."

Nick was scanning the file closely. Johnson had added his own printout on the drug. Ketamine was tasteless and colorless. Nick's mind was racing. So, someone might have put the drug on or in her mouthpiece. They would have had to do it right before the dive. Did she leave from the beach? Was she diving from a boat? Did the other person dive with her? And the biggest question of all: how did that damned van Gogh play into all of this? He rubbed his temples with the thumb and index finger of his dry hand then gulped his coffee.

"Yeah, you're thinking what I'm thinking," said Johnson. "They must have had access to her equipment not long before she went on the dive. But I don't think they dove with her because they didn't take the painting. She still had it."

"Let's take a walk. Actually, let's go back to the beach where we found her. I want to think this through from the beginning." Nick downed the last of his coffee, crushed the paper cup with one hand and tossed it across the room toward the trashcan. He missed.

Half an hour later Nick Black and Adam Johnson stood on the small beach where they had found Jennifer Hully. The sun was setting. Calm, mild weather had resulted in a low, gentle surf lapping the shore. Johnson put his hands on his hips. "Kinda romantic. Too bad for you I'm married."

Nick just rolled his eyes. He walked over to the large rock outcropping where they had found the body. "So she was on ketamine, probably hallucinating. That means she probably wasn't paying attention to her air supply."

"She might have been passed out," Johnson piped in.

Nick shook his head. "I don't think so. I think her mouthpiece would have come out if that was the case and her tank wouldn't have necessarily drained. She'd still have drowned, but with air left in the tank. No, I think she was awake and breathing but had no clue where she was or what she was doing. She kept breathing and seeing, well, who knows what she was seeing, or thought she saw, and finally she ran out of air. If that happened, would she have panicked when she ran out, or would she just have taken one big gulp of water and… lights out?"

"Don't know. Don't know as I'd ever want to know. But it sure did look like plain ol' lights out to me."

"Yeah, me too."

Johnson picked up a rock and, leaning over with a groan, skipped it across the water. He stood up straight again with another louder groan. "Oh, the joints! Gettin' old ya know." Nick just snorted in response.

"All right, guess we better get home. I'm sure you have supper on the table," Nick said.

Adam Johnson grinned and rubbed his hands together. "Oohh yeah! Tonight's fish fry! Takes a full week to get the smell outta the house, then we do it all over again. I could eat a dozen!"

"I don't doubt that," said Nick as they got back in the car.

Nick dropped off his partner at the police station then went back home. His apartment was a small studio in one of the old brick buildings near the waterfront. They called that section of the city the Old Port. Once seedy and undesirable, it had been gentrified and was now the hot spot for trendy restaurants and weekend nightlife. Unfortunately, this had kept Nick awake on many a Friday and Saturday night. He'd thought of moving several times but never seemed to take the steps to find a new place. Besides, the price was right and it was convenient to the station.

He threw his keys on the kitchen counter and grabbed a bottle of wine. It was his one indulgence.

He'd fallen into wine collecting as a hobby several years earlier and hadn't stopped. This one was a lovely Pinot Noir from the Russian River Valley near San Francisco. He had vowed to go there someday but hadn't been able to fit it in his schedule. Yet. He pulled the cork out and poured a glass.

Dulcie collected wines too, he thought. He remembered a conversation they'd once had. He really wanted to talk to her. Would that seem strange? It had only been a couple of hours since he'd seen her last.

However, there was the issue of the van Gogh that he had yet to mention to her. Of course the Feds had jumped in on that one. They loved art thefts. Very high profile and it made them look good to solve those cases. He'd had to turn the canvas over to them right away, although that didn't stop him from doing a little research on his own.

He sat at the small table that served as both a dining area and a desk and pulled open his laptop. '*Where to start?*' he thought. He stood up again, yanked his shirt out of the waist of his jeans, unbuckled his belt and pulled it out of the pant loops in one easy motion. Slinging it on the bed in the corner of the room, he sat down again.

"Ok, let's see what we can find out about the theft of that thing," he said out loud. An hour later he'd compiled a respectable file of information. The painting had belonged to an investment banker, or more accurately, his wife, as he'd bought it for her as a gift. It had sold for a mere three-quarters of a million dollars. "Some gift," Nick muttered. He reached for his wine and discovered the glass was empty. '*Another half wouldn't kill me,*' he thought.

Pouring a second full glass he glanced at the clock on the stove. Eight-thirty.

A soft knock on the door made him jump. '*Who the hell...?*' he thought. No one ever came to see him. He looked through the peephole, drew back quickly, shoved his shirttails into his jeans as neatly as possible, and opened the door.

Dulcie looked up at him. "I'm sorry to just come by. I should have called first. I can come back later. It's just that I was thinking, and I'd been out walking. It's such a nice night. And I remember you'd told me that you lived here..." She trailed off.

He was speechless for a moment. He gripped the doorknob hard to regain his composure. Then he stepped back, gesturing her in, and said, "No, not at all. That's fine. Come in." She walked in and saw the full glass on the table.

"Are you having wine?" Dulcie asked, then winced inwardly. She didn't want him to think she was asking for some or that she wanted to stay any length of time.

"Yeah. It's my most heinous indulgence. Here, have some." He stepped into the kitchen area and quickly poured another glass. He held it out to her.

"I'm sorry," she said without taking it. "I really don't want to impose. I just can't stop thinking about..."

"Take the damned glass so I can drink mine," he said, smiling.

She grinned sheepishly. "Yes. Thank you! But wait till my friends hear that an officer of the law forced alcohol on me!" She took the glass and glanced into the apartment. The van Gogh was in full view on the laptop.

"Hey, that's the van Gogh that was stolen last year! Are you working on that case too?" she asked walking over to the table.

Nick took a deep breath. In spite of the Feds telling him to keep it quiet, he knew he had to tell her. "You could say that." He pulled out a chair for her at the table. "There's more to the Jennifer Hully death than what you currently know." Dulcie's eyes widened but she was silent. "You have to promise not to reveal anything that I'm about to tell you."

Dulcie almost laughed at how solemn he looked but then realized just how serious he was. "Of course," she murmured.

Nick sat down and leaned toward her. "When we found Jennifer Hully's body washed up on the beach, we also found a watertight tube with her. Inside the tube was this painting."

Dulcie opened her mouth to speak. Nothing came out except a small cracking noise. She closed her mouth again, then took a gulp of wine.

"Yeah, I know. The FBI took over that part of the case immediately. They have the painting and are testing it to see if it's genuine."

"If it's in a watertight tube and it shows up with a dead woman, isn't it safe to say that it's probably genuine?"

Nick smiled. "I get your point. But you of all people know that it has to be tested."

Dulcie shifted sideways in her chair and put her arm on the table. She toyed with the glass, slowly spinning it around, watching the wine coat the clear sides. "Absolutely. Yes, of course. That puts everything into a whole new category though, doesn't it?"

Nick nodded. "I wanted to tell you but the Feds tied my hands. I'm not supposed to be discussing it with anyone. But I'm at my wit's end trying to figure this out."

"So let me get this straight. Jennifer Hully washes up on the beach. She's drowned by accident."

Nick cut her off. "OK, that's the other thing that I haven't mentioned. It looks like it wasn't an accident."

Dulcie stared at him. "Seriously?"

"Yeah, seriously. The coroner found ketamine in her saliva."

"And ketamine is..."

"Basically it's a kind of anesthesia but it's also a hallucinogenic drug."

"Wow." Dulcie took a long sip of her pinot noir and let it roll around in her mouth. At last she swallowed, held up the glass and said, "This is really good! Russian River Valley?"

Nick was stunned. She was way out of his league if she knew that from tasting. He just nodded, his eyes wide.

Dulcie burst out laughing. "I saw the bottle, silly. I'm not that good!" She turned back to the computer screen. "So, Jennifer had this painting with her when she washed up on the beach. That means that if someone killed her, they didn't know what was in the tube. Or, they didn't even know there was a tube. Her sister swears that she always followed safety precautions and dove with a buddy. Either her buddy drugged her and took off, but Jennifer located the tube in the meantime before the drug took effect, or someone drugged her beforehand, then she went diving alone to retrieve the tube, and died. Either way, the person who drugged her didn't know about the canvas, right?" Dulcie had been speaking rapid-fire, trying to keep up with her thoughts.

Nick hesitated. He pictured each scenario. She was right.

"And Nick, this actually makes more sense now. Remember that I told you I felt Lydia flinch when we mentioned the phone number? If her sister was involved in some kind of art theft or fraud and Lydia knew about it, she would be nervous, especially if she thought that Jennifer would be talking to me or anyone else. I know I would be."

Nick nodded. "That does make sense. That could mean that Lydia knows more than she's telling us. I need to talk to her again. I'll head over there in the morning."

"Do you know anything more about the drug she was given? Was it ketamine, did you say?"

"Yes. I don't know much more. It isn't common, and it really isn't used much as a recreational drug. It's mostly an anesthetic and seems to be used as much by vets as regular doctors."

"So that means it could actually be more easily available," said Dulcie. "And it was found in her saliva. Did you test her equipment?"

Nick chuckled. "Want to be on police staff? That's the first thing I asked, too. The lab is doing that now."

Dulcie put down her now empty glass. "Well, it looks like we won't have any answers until tomorrow at the earliest. I should get home. Thanks so much for the wine. And the chat." She stood up.

"I can run you home. It's too late to walk by yourself."

"No, I don't want to be any trouble. Besides, it's a beautiful night. And I have complete faith in the Portland Police Department to keep the streets safe."

"Even still. I'll walk you home. You'll have personalized service from the Portland Police force. You can't say no to that."

Dulcie laughed and allowed him to steer her out the door.

*I dream of painting and then
I paint my dream.*
~ Vincent van Gogh

CHAPTER EIGHT

Lexi Kent always assumed that she wasn't a jealous woman, until Clark Davenport-Jones married someone else. It wasn't as though she really wanted to marry him. Or could for that matter. But the thought of him going home to a wife did not sit well.

The fact that she was now in her thirties was unsettling. She still looked fabulous, she was very careful to make sure of that, but Clark's wandering eye had not escaped her attention. She had even seen it wander at his own wedding reception to his new wife's attractive and daredevil sister. Lexi had wondered if she should cause some mischief regarding that, but decided to keep it to herself. Better to use it as a trump card at some future date, if necessary. Besides, she couldn't make waves. She had a past as well, and one secret in particular could be played either for or against her. She had to be careful so that she could use it to her advantage.

For now she had to keep a relatively low profile. This annoyed her constantly. She had to stay busy or she would think about it too much. '*I'll go for a ride,*' she thought. That would kill a few hours and she always felt better afterward.

Lexi had learned to ride in an English saddle when she was very young, as did most of the girls that were in her elite private school. She had owned her own horse since she was a teenager and stabled him with her uncle, Donald Winters. Lexi pulled on her snug jodhpurs, an even snugger polo shirt, and smiled at herself in the mirror. She brushed her golden hair back into a low ponytail. For now, she slipped on her Wellies—they were easier to drive in than her stiff riding boots. These she threw into a large canvas bag along with gloves, helmet, and a small bag of carrots. Hadrian loved carrots.

The day was sunny and warm. She sped north toward Winterhaven Stables and arrived sooner than she anticipated. She gave a warm smile to the stable attendant, a handsome young man in his twenties, and made her way back to Hadrian's stall.

Lexi took a deep breath. The smell of the hay and, although she would never admit it, horse dung, always seemed to calm her. She reached into her bag, pulled out a carrot, and watched Hadrian happily munching. It was then that she realized someone was in the next stall.

"That's it girl. I know, you don't like it. Don't worry. You won't feel bad for long. I'll make it all better soon." The voice was calm and soothing. Lexi couldn't remember which horse was in the next stall, but something told her to be quiet. She peeked through a crack between the wide wooden slats of the stable wall. All she could see was the back of a man's head as he bent down beside the horse. He had a syringe in his hand. He patted the horse, a beautiful chestnut mare, and softly whispered to her. Lexi couldn't hear what he was saying. He put the syringe back in his bag, clicked it shut, and strode out of the stable.

Lexi stepped out and looked at the stall next to Hadrian's. Yes, that's right. It was Attagirl. She remembered hearing about the thoroughbred's racing career and gazed admiringly at her. '*She must be sick right now*,' thought Lexi.

Putting it out of her mind, she walked through the stable to retrieve her saddle. As she rounded the corner she ran nearly headlong into the man she had just seen in Attagirl's stall. He looked surprised to see anyone.

"Oh, I'm so sorry," said Lexi. "I wasn't paying attention."

"No, not at all. My apologies." He stepped beyond her but went into a different stall this time. Lexi had the feeling that he was trying to avoid her. She took her time getting the saddle until she saw him leave again. Something seemed strange about him. She was unsettled enough to call to the stable hand and have him help her ready Hadrian for her ride. Besides, she liked having him assist her into the saddle.

Ross Davenport-Jones sat in his Land Rover until he saw Lexi trot from the stable grounds. Then he quietly got out again and hiked across the large grassy yard to the main house. He rang the bell. The housekeeper knew him well and led him in. "I'll get Mr. Winters for you sir. He'll be happy to see you."

Donald Winters looked nothing like an outdoors enthusiast, because he was not. He loved horses but hadn't been on one for years. He was short, with a barrel-shaped torso, two more barrels for legs, barrel arms, and large sausages for hands. Although he was reasonably fit, he resembled a taller man that had been smushed in from all sides.

"Jonsey, you old fool!" he boomed and stuck out a meaty hand for Ross to shake. Ross tried not to wince as his hand was squeezed hard. "Didn't know you were here!" Donald Winters continued, still squeezing.

"I was passing by and thought I'd check up on your mares. Looks like your young girl may foal, but Attagirl just didn't take. Again." He watched Winters closely.

The stout man rubbed the top of his head with his big hand. "Well, there goes that stud fee," he said. "I don't know, Jonsey. She may be more trouble than it's worth. C'mon in and have a drink with me. Let's talk it over."

Ross followed him into his office, which was probably the original library of the large house. It was lined with shelves, but they held few books. Instead, Donald Winters had propped up framed photos of numerous horses along with trophies and awards stuffed among them. Each horse had at least a single shelf to itself, while some had an entire bookcase. The shelf edges were trimmed haphazardly with ribbons and badges. It gave the entire room a somewhat juvenile, feminine look, as though a little girl had decorated with pictures of her favorite ponies.

Ross sat down in the green leather chair opposite Winter's large oak desk. Donald Winters nestled into his burgundy leather office chair, rocking back and forth, his feet swinging slightly above the floor. He gestured toward a bottle of single malt, which Ross was all too happy to pour. He slid a glass across the desk to Winters and took one for himself.

Sitting back in the chair Ross could barely see Winters' face over the top of the desk. But the man was thinking hard and did not seem to notice. Ross gently changed his position so that he was sitting up a bit higher. He needed to read the man well right now.

Donald Winters downed the expensive whiskey in one gulp and set down the glass hard on his desk. "Well, Jonsey," he shouted. "She's been good to me, but it's probably time I guess." He gazed up at the shelves with Attagirl's awards and trophies. "Yep, I think it's time. Guess I should put her on the block. Whattaya think she's worth?"

Ross took a long sip of his drink. "Well, if she can't produce a foal at this point she isn't worth much. Some rich father with a guilt complex might buy her for his kid." He was careful only to imply that she currently couldn't breed. He didn't want to say outright that she was barren.

Winters nodded. "Odd, though. She did breed before. But she is gettin' older so who can tell?" Then he laughed loudly. "Other than you, Jonsey!"

Ross smiled. "I couldn't even say for sure. You never know. But I don't think she's much of a sure thing any longer."

"Nope. Loved her like a daughter, I did. But a man's gotta make a living. All right, I'll get the paperwork together. Can you get her medical records ready?" he boomed.

Ross finished his drink and put the glass back on the silver plate next to the whiskey bottle. He stood up. "I'll get right on it," he said quietly.

"Good. Might have a buyer already you know. A lady inquired about her recently. I laughed and said Attagirl wasn't for sale. Guess she knew something I didn't!"

Ross said nothing. He simply shook Donald Winter's outstretched hand again and quickly saw himself out.

ଓଃ

"Hmmm, …van Gogh, …van Gogh, vanGogh vanGoghvanGogh," Dulcie muttered as she punched at the keys on her computer. She was looking for more information on the theft. An investment banker had bought it for his wife. They had it hanging in their apartment in Boston, which was on the eighth floor of a highly secure building.

One day the wife came home and the painting was missing. Simply an empty space left on the wall. No one could figure it out. The building management had been thoroughly questioned, as had the cleaning company that came in weekly. There were no leads.

"So why would it end up at the bottom of the ocean?" said Dulcie. "Or at least, in a tube that had been in the ocean?" She wondered about that. On the one hand, it was the perfect hiding place. Chances were extremely slim that anyone would come across it if it were somehow anchored on the sea floor. On the other hand, it was ridiculously risky for so many reasons.

Dulcie realized that she didn't know exactly where Jennifer's body had washed up. Nick had just said that it was in Cape Elizabeth. She pulled up a map and a depth chart on her computer. Not really any clues there. She'd have to ask Nick.

Nick. That was an interesting situation. She knew that she liked him, that she was attracted to him. They got along very well. He had an easy, familiar manner that made her feel safe and comfortable. He seemed interested in her, but he was very reserved too. Odd.

She also found it odd that he lived in such a small apartment. Barely more than a room. It had the kitchen that was separate, and a bathroom of course. As a detective he surely must be making a decent salary but clearly he wasn't spending it on living arrangements. Then again, he was a guy, and having grown up with a brother, she knew that they often didn't really care about where or how they lived. She smiled. Men were strange like that.

Dulcie picked up her cell phone and scrolled through the contacts. She found Nick's name and pressed the call button. "Hey, Dulcie." He'd answered so quickly she didn't know exactly what she was going to say. "Dulcie? That is you, isn't it?"

Dulcie laughed. "Sorry, I was thinking. Quick question. Where exactly did Jennifer wash up on the beach? I mean, which beach?"

"It's the one over at Kettle Cove. Do you know it?"

"Yup, I know exactly which one. Now that's really strange."

"What's strange about it?"

"Kettle Cove is an incredibly popular dive spot. Every time I've gone there I've seen at least one other pair of divers, usually a lot more than that. They even have classes out there sometimes."

"OK, but why is that strange?"

"Well, if she was diving in that area, why would she have the tube with the painting? She'd run the risk of easily being seen."

"Yes, but no one would have known what was inside so maybe she didn't think it was a risk? And she was a risk-taker."

"True. Good point."

"Plus it wasn't really that big. About eighteen inches long and two or three inches in diameter. The painting was pretty small," Nick said.

"So she could have grabbed it and just kept it close. Or even stuffed it inside her buoyancy vest."

"Yes. Visibility down there isn't that great even on a good day, so if other divers were around, there's still a good chance that the tube wouldn't have been seen."

"It's possible," said Dulcie. "But why was she alone? Whoever killed her must have had access to her equipment just before she dove. So they either dove with her and just left her, or they were on the beach— or boat—that she dove from. Which reminds me, did your guys find the drug on her equipment?"

"Yes, as we expected. There were traces of it on her mouthpiece. Along with a water-soluble kind of wax which would have held it in place for long enough so that it reached her mouth rather than washing off. They even found some on her snorkel. Whoever did it was thorough."

"My bet is that they dove with her. Maybe it was even a night dive. I don't like doing those but I have a couple of times. If people don't have lights on, you can lose them pretty easily. It's even difficult to see land again sometimes if the mist comes in. We had people on the beach with a bright light both of the times that I went. Some people love it, but I feel too nervous and disoriented."

"That's a really good point, Dulcie. They could have put the drug on her mouthpiece, gone in with her, then ditched her part way through. She may have even started to feel disoriented from the ketamine, but as you said that isn't entirely unusual on a night dive."

"And they may not have known that she was going to pick up a tube with a painting in it. She may have just told some kind of story about getting something that she'd left behind earlier. Or she even could have taken it while they weren't looking. That would be easy enough."

"So why did she have it, and why was she killed?" Nick said. It was probably the hundredth time he'd had that thought.

"And we're right back at the beginning again," Dulcie replied. "OK, that was fun," she said with a bit of sarcasm. She heard Nick sigh on the other end of the line. "I'll stop pestering you," she said, "and let you get back to solving the case."

Nick tried to sound lighthearted. "Yeah, thanks. I'm making great progress," he said facetiously. "Talk to you later."

Nick had been sitting in his car while he talked with Dulcie. He had just left the home of Lydia Davenport-Jones, and was getting annoyed with the lack of information. She knew almost nothing about her sister's personal life. She said that they spoke once or twice per month on average, and usually about trivial topics or family issues. Nick had managed to slide questions about art into the conversation in reference to Dulcie's cell phone number on Jennifer's hand, but Lydia simply shook her head and said that she had no idea.

He didn't believe her. Nothing that she said or did gave him any reason *not* to believe her. But he didn't. It was his sixth sense as a detective, the instinctive moment when he knew something wasn't right. It was what made him so good at his job.

Nick started the car again and pulled it back out onto the road. He decided to go back to where Jennifer had been found. Again. He had been there with Johnson, but this time he wanted to be alone. He had to think.

Nick drove along the winding roads from Prouts Neck around the coast to Cape Elizabeth. He turned into Kettle Cove and parked in the small public lot. It was a cool day, and the lot was mostly empty. Leaving the car, he walked onto the small beach and looked out at the ocean. He imagined what it would be like after dark, in the cold blackness. Pretty scary, he thought. Unless you were hallucinating and seeing mermaids.

The phone number. That one stumped him too. He thought that Lydia might have known something more about it, but after questioning her, he did believe that it had come as a surprise to her as well.

He had to find someone else who knew Jennifer. She couldn't have been that much of a lone wolf. She couldn't have been working alone. And for that matter, she must have been supporting herself somehow. She must have worked or done something for money. Nick had done his homework on the Hully family and they certainly weren't well off.

'*When I get back to the station,*' he thought, '*I'll check the databases. She must have worked somewhere. Her name has to pop up on something.*' He hoped, more than believed, that it would.

As Nicholas Black was gazing out at the ocean, Dan Chambers and his first mate Freddie were gazing back in. They had a boat full of happy tourists and were lazily making their way back around the cape. Normally Nick didn't take this route, but the wind and tide had been right, so he decided to give it a try. His passengers didn't really care, and he and Freddie needed the change of scenery.

Freddie leaned over the back of the yacht then yelled up to Dan. "Cap'n! Sorry, but ya just hooked one I think."

Dan cursed under his breath and threw the engine into neutral. Smiling at the passengers, he said, "Sorry. It'll take just a minute. We get hooked up on lobster buoys once in a while."

"How 'bout we snag one for supper!" said a man toward the front. Everyone laughed.

"No can do. Lobstermen are pretty territorial. They carry rifles just in case someone even thinks about their catch."

The man put up both hands in surrender and the passengers laughed again.

Dan joined Freddie, who pointed at the buoy. "Got her good, looks like." Dan exhaled loudly, grabbed the boat hook, and started disentangling the buoy. He hoped that he wouldn't have to actually get in the water to get it free. Freddie watched him. "Funny the colors. That one's different from these others."

Dan didn't pay much attention to him. After a few minutes of tugging, it came loose. He watched it drift in the current away from the yacht. At that point, Freddie's words sank in. It was different. It was gold and black while all the others in the area were orange and blue or yellow and red. He looked around for more buoys with the same gold and black pattern but saw none. "Yeah, you're right Freddie. That is weird."

Freddie's obsessive nature took over. "Cap'n, lets go back and check the numbering. We should see who has that one. Maybe they don't know how to set it right?"

Dan looked back at the buoy slowly drifting. "No, we don't really have time. No big deal anyway."

"It does seem odd to have the different one," said Freddie. "We should check."

Dan shook his head. "Really Freddie, we don't have time. We need to get these folks home." Freddie's obsessive nature was usually helpful to keep everything *ship-shape* as he would often say, but at times it could get annoying. "All set!" Dan announced to the passengers. A collective cheer went up.

Back at the helm, Dan grew more curious about the markings. As the son and grandson of a fisherman and lobsterman, he knew just about everything there was to know about the industry. He knew never to touch anyone's traps. He knew how the lines were set. And he knew how to steer clear of them for that reason too, which was exactly why this trap did not make sense. He was running between the lines, and should not have been caught up on anything. He had not caught any of the others. This was a lone trap that did not seem to be set properly. It was probably crossing someone else's line too, which they would not be happy about.

"Probably a recreational guy who doesn't have a clue what he's doing," Dan muttered to himself. The state issued a few recreational licenses but typically those traps were not among the commercial ones. The amateurs were cautioned to steer clear of the pros.

Dan knew it would continue to bother him. He also knew that Freddie was not about to let the subject drop, either. He glanced at the shore, noting landmarks. He would be back to check it out, he was sure. No time right now, however. The trip back to Portland Harbor would be long enough.

As he steered the boat back into the harbor at last, the passengers rustled about getting their things together. Dan watched Freddie moving among them, collecting trash, chatting, making sure they had a good time. He knew that Freddie was a find, but evidently it was a sentiment that Freddie's wife did not agree with completely. *'Guess they had different priorities for marriage back then,'* he thought. *'Compatibility was not necessarily one of them.'*

An artist never really finishes his work;
he merely abandons it.
~ Paul Valéry

CHAPTER NINE

When Amelia Davenport-Jones wanted something, she always got it. Sometimes it would take years, but once in her sights, she never quit the hunt. The Maine Museum of Art's little Micronesian ceremonial bowl was now clearly in her sights. She knew the auction estimate from the previous year, before the piece had been withdrawn. It had been in the catalog. She saved that catalog, carefully bookmarking the page. She had looked at it nearly every day since.

Amelia had planned to contact the museum's previous director, Joshua Harriman, whom she knew well from social circles. From the bit of sleuthing she had done, she learned that he had instigated the idea of auctioning the piece to raise funds. He had convinced the board but then they had a change of heart. She was going to approach him personally about it but then the damned fool went and got himself killed. She shook her head, annoyed with the thought of having to start all over again cultivating a relationship with the new museum director, Dr. Chambers.

The lunch had gone fairly well. She had presented her idea of buying the work. Dr. Chambers seemed receptive. Yet she hinted at a condition that annoyed Amelia. If she bought the work, she would be required to lend it to the museum for display at least twice over the following five years. It seemed that they had two exhibits on the long-term schedule that were excellent venues for the little bowl. Amelia did not like this. Once she owned a work, it was hers. She wanted complete control. She usually kept newly purchased items hidden away for some time so that only she could see them whenever she liked. This condition of the sale was not acceptable.

Amelia was just about to leave her Beacon Hill townhouse when she was startled by the buzzing of her cell phone. "I cannot get used to that damned thing!" she said out loud. Then, grabbing it from her purse she yelled, "HELLO?"

"Mom, it's me. Stop yelling," Clark Davenport-Jones had told her hundreds of times that the phone wasn't a walkie-talkie or a short-wave radio. It was just like a regular phone in her house. "Just speak normally, Mom," he had said over and over again. It never did sink in.

"CLARK! What is it? Where are you?" Amelia did not have a high opinion of small talk.

"Mom, I'm at home. Listen Mom, I have some bad news. It's about Lydia."

Amelia's heart jumped. Maybe Lydia had been in a bad accident. Or she had a terminal illness. Or maybe she'd had an affair and Clark was divorcing her! "WHAT?" shouted Amelia.

"It's actually Lydia's sister, Jennifer. She died a few days ago. It was a scuba diving accident. They found her on a beach over in Cape Elizabeth. Lydia is pretty devastated. The funeral is in two days, on Saturday. I thought I'd let you know in case you or Dad wanted to be there."

Amelia paused, pulling the phone away from her head and looking at it for a moment through squinted eyes. Then she put it back to her ear. "Why on earth would we be there?" she yelled.

Clark was silent. Then he quietly said, "To show a bit of support for my wife, perhaps?"

Amelia heard the line click. She looked at her phone. *Call Ended*, it read. She sat down on the chair in the front hall of her home, staring at the phone. Her mind was working quickly, trying to make the right connections. Lydia's sister. Jennifer. She had seen Ross talking with her at Clark's wedding reception. Ross didn't think that she noticed anything that he did, but she made it a point to be aware of everything. She hadn't liked the liaison then and she liked it even less as time went on. Was liaison too strong a word? No, it seemed appropriate given how they looked when she saw them together. Or at least it was appropriate for the way Ross looked. The girl had seemed very cool and controlled. Interesting.

Amelia heard a key in the door and stood up from her chair, pretending to dig in her purse. She looked up as Ross came through. He seemed a bit startled to see her. She remembered that the last time they had been together she had slapped him. She had to hold back a nasty smile thinking about it.

"Ross, dear. I just got off the phone with Clark. It seems we'll have to go to a funeral on Saturday. Lydia's sister died."

It was as though she had slapped him again. His face grew white and he groped for the chair beside him. He sat down quickly, trying to regain his composure.

"Is anything wrong, Ross? You look as white as a sheet," Amelia said with feigned concern.

"No, no. I've been having these headaches that come over me quickly. What was it you said? Lydia's sister?"

"Yes Ross. She's dead. Some kind of swimming accident, I think. Clark wants us to come to the funeral, although I can't understand why."

Ross nodded. He swallowed hard several times. "Where is it?" he asked at last.

Amelia laughed. "You know, I didn't think to ask. Why don't you give Clark a call and find out the details. I'm stepping out for a bit. Must get to the gallery before it closes to pick up my new Albers. They've framed it beautifully!" She grabbed her purse and sauntered out the door.

Ross sat in silence after the door closed. He felt sick. It was all going so wrong. Why had he started all of this in the first place? Ross Davenport-Jones was not the type to pull off clandestine deals and underhanded deeds. He did not have the stomach for it. Nor the heart for that matter, he realized as the pounding in his chest had yet to subside. Now what?

He pulled himself up to a standing position again, waiting for several seconds to make sure that his legs would hold him up properly. Then he slowly shuffled into the study. He opened the liquor cabinet and poured himself a hefty measure of brandy. It was the second time that day that he had imbibed in something strong. This business was going to ruin him in more ways than one.

Sinking into the nearest chair, he rested the glass on the arm and listened to the clock ticking. It was calming. He didn't know how long he had been sitting there. Suddenly, he heard a car horn from outside. It made him jump, spilling what was left of his brandy.

"I don't know what to do," he whispered. Then he realized that there was nothing he could do at this point. He had to remain calm. "I'll call Clark. Maybe if I have more details I'll be able to figure out what's next." He reached in his pocket for his phone.

Clark answered almost immediately. "Dad," he said. "You've heard?"

Ross nodded then realized Clark couldn't see him. "Yes, your mother just told me. How'd it happen?"

"The police said it was a diving accident. Scuba diving. Jennifer always was doing things like that. They said she ran out of air."

"Yikes. Tough way to go, I'd imagine," said Ross, not knowing how to reply.

"I have no idea. I don't want to know. Dad, Lydia is pretty shaken by it. I've had the doctor in to see her. She had to identify Jennifer in the morgue too. It was awful. The strange thing is that she swears Jennifer would never go diving alone. We can't figure out why someone wouldn't have at least reported her missing if they'd lost track of her during the dive."

"That is a mystery. Very strange," said Ross.

"Anyway, the funeral is on Saturday. It's at St. Mary's, the Episcopalian one, in Scarborough. At eleven. Do you and Mom think you can make it? I know Lydia would appreciate it."

"Yes, we'll certainly be there. Of course."

"Thanks, Dad. She needs everyone's support right now. Oh, I hear her upstairs. She was napping. I'll go see how she's doing. Bye, Dad."

"Bye, Clark."

Ross put the phone back in his pocket. He should have tried to find out more. How did they find her? Where did they find her? He'd have to ask around at the funeral.

☘

A soft mist had made its way slowly from the water, over the beach, and finally reached Lydia Davenport-Jones's upstairs window. She had been awake and watching it for quite some time. It diffused the low afternoon light, surrounding the cottage with a strange yellow glow.

Lydia had been thinking about Jennifer. Of course she had been thinking about Jennifer. There was little else that she could think about. But to keep her mind from focusing on the nightmare of being in cold water and not having air to breathe, she forced herself to think about Jennifer's hand. The hand with the telephone number.

When she had gone to the morgue she had seen Jennifer's face. She looked peaceful although extremely pale. Lydia remembered thinking that she had never actually seen Jennifer pale before. She was outdoors so much that her skin always had at least some degree of suntan. Then she remembered what the policeman had said about her hand.

The morgue attendant had looked at her strangely when she asked to see Jennifer's hands but he had gently pulled them out from under the sheet. Lydia had thought it was nice that he was so gentle. As though he was trying not to wake her.

It was the left hand. Jennifer was right handed, so she could have written the number herself. But the longer Lydia looked at it, the more she thought that it was not Jennifer's writing. '*Maybe I'm just fooling myself,*' she thought. '*After all, if you write on your own hand, how much like your own writing could it possibly look?*'

Lydia thought about Dr. Chambers. She vaguely remembered her from school, years before. Dulcie had always been very smart and very quiet. '*It's the quiet ones you have to look out for,*' she thought. '*And maybe she isn't so quiet any more?*' For Jennifer to contact Dulcie would have been a huge risk, if it was to talk about anything related to art. Jennifer did love her risks, though.

Life beats down and crushes the soul
and art reminds you that you have one.
~ Stella Adler

CHAPTER TEN

Nicholas Black had attended far too many funerals, mostly for people that he had never even met. This was no different. He could tell at a glance who was truly sad, who would miss her, who was there to support someone else, and who would stay only for the minimum amount of time because it was expected. And there was often another person, sometimes more than one, that fell into one final group: those who liked to stir up trouble. Usually they were involved with the will in some way, but not always. Sometimes they were looking for justification, vindication, even revenge.

He stood quietly on the side of the church, in the shadow of a column, not moving. "What do you see, Detective?" The whisper brushed his ear and made him jump. He froze again, but turned his head slightly to see Dulcie standing in the shadows behind him.

"You'd make a good undercover cop, you know," he murmured. She snorted softly in reply.

Again, without moving, he said, "Third row, on the left. The older couple. Know them?"

Dulcie leaned forward. Her chin was nearly on his shoulder. "That's Amelia and Ross Davenport-Jones. Clark's parents. Good of them to come." She glanced at him curiously. "I thought you knew them vaguely, too?"

"It's been years. I was pretty sure it was them though. Just checking. Do you know Lydia and Jennifer's parents? Would you recognize them?"

"Not at all. But they shouldn't be hard to figure out."

Nick nodded. "I should go sit. I'm too conspicuous here. Especially with you peering over my shoulder like that." He turned to face her and rolled his eyes.

"Decorum, Detective! This is a funeral, after all," she whispered. They found seats in the very back of the church.

"If anyone sees me here who knows me, they might wonder why I'm here," Nick said. "No one is aware that it's a murder investigation. Except you, that is."

"And the murderer," Dulcie said.

"Good point," Nick replied. "But they don't know that I know. Or that you know. And I'd rather keep it that way for now." They sat silently, watching people filter into the long pews, nod somber greetings to each other, and quietly take their seats.

The service lasted for only half an hour. Toward the end, Dulcie was vaguely aware of someone entering late. She heard, rather than saw, a brief flurry of activity in the pew on the opposite side. Nick sat between her and the latecomer. She saw him glance over, and could have sworn that has face had gone pale.

After the service guests were invited to Clark and Lydia's home. Jennifer's body was being taken to a crematorium where another, smaller service was to be held the next day. Dulcie offered Nick a ride to the beachfront cottage. "Thanks, but let's take my car," he said. "Unfortunately, I have to be available for a quick exit should duty call." He drove smoothly along the winding roads toward the ocean.

As it came into view, Dulcie smiled. "Funny," she said. "It's the same water, but it just depends on the house you're in beside it, or the boat you're in on it."

Nick glanced at her. "What do you mean?"

"My family lived on the water, but not like this," she gestured at the grand houses of the rich around her. "I come from a line of fishermen and lobstermen. I was the fifth generation to live in that house. I watched my dad go out on a boat nearly every day. But it wasn't a boat like that, for sure!" She pointed to a beautiful sailboat slipping along through the sunlight, clearly there simply to give pleasure. "It's strange how the exact same thing can be different, depending on who you are."

Nick nodded. He didn't think she remembered when he had mentioned his own background once before. He had been one of those people. The ones who lived in the houses that they drove by now. And he had walked away from it all.

Dulcie turned to him. "Do you know who came into the church late? I heard someone but couldn't see them." She saw his hand grip the steering wheel tighter. *'Did I strike a nerve?'* she thought. *'Or did I just change the subject too suddenly?'*

"A friend of Clark's, I think," he replied. "From Boston. Do you know if it's going to stay sunny today or are showers coming in like yesterday?"

Dulcie almost laughed out loud. For such an excellent police detective, his change of subject was ridiculously obvious. "I really don't know. Ah, here we are. Looks like nearly everyone else is here already." They drove slowly for some distance before finding a place to pull over and park. Dulcie stepped out of the car, glad that she'd worn her flats for the walk to Clark and Lydia's cottage.

The room was full when they arrived. People were standing, drinking coffee, holding finger sandwiches or cookies on napkins but not actually eating anything. Some were perched on the arm of a sofa or leaning against the barstools but no one actually sat. Dulcie wondered why that was always the case. Maybe they didn't want anyone, including themselves, to think they were staying for long? She leaned toward Nick. "I'll get you a coffee. What do you take?" She saw him scanning the room.

"Cream. Thanks. I'll be over there." He nodded to the corner beside the fireplace mantle. He could see straight through to the kitchen from there. For the umpteenth time, he wished that he could read lips. *'I've gotta learn that,'* he thought. In his spare time. Sure.

Dulcie located the coffee in the kitchen. As she was pouring she sensed someone beside her and looked up.

"I didn't expect to see you here," said Amelia Davenport-Jones.

'Dammit,' thought Dulcie. She hadn't thought to cook up a cover story with Nick. "A friend from a

long time ago. I went to high school with Lydia and Jennifer," said Dulcie.

"Ah yes," Amelia replied smoothly, looking Dulcie up and down. "Small world. " She turned to leave and bumped into a man standing behind her. Dulcie saw a quick look of disgust flash across her face. She forced a smile and said, "Ms. Chambers, have you met my husband? This is Ross."

The man stuck out his hand with a jerky motion. He shook Dulcie's exactly once, then released it quickly. "Pleased to meet you," he added quietly.

Dulcie smiled warmly at him. "You also. Your wife and I have a great deal in common, both lovers of the art world," she said.

Ross looked pained. "Yes, that's a good way to put it."

Amelia grabbed his arm and said, "We have to talk to Clark." Without even looking at Dulcie, she pulled him into the next room.

'Wow,' thought Dulcie. 'There's a match made in Hell.'

Dulcie followed them at a distance to rejoin Nick. She stopped short and nearly spilled the coffee when she saw him talking with someone. Dulcie had never seen her before. She was striking. Blonde, heels that were a little too high for the occasion, expensive clothes. She was turned away from Dulcie, so she couldn't see the woman's face. She could see Nick's, however. He clearly was not happy.

Dulcie pretended to admire the ocean view, and timed her trip across the living room so that she reached Nick just after the woman left. "Who was that?" she asked. "You didn't look happy to see her."

Nick looked tense. He took a deep breath. "Her family and mine were friends. In Boston. We kind of grew up together. Actually the families are still friends, but I've been shunned since I chose not to follow the predestined path."

"I'm surprised she talked to you then," said Dulcie, handing him his coffee.

"Yeah," he muttered. He took a big gulp. It was hot, thankfully. Coffee was usually lukewarm at best for these gatherings. He was grateful. It cleared his throat along with his thinking.

'She was the one who came in late,' Dulcie thought. *'No wonder he didn't like seeing her. He's working right now. He doesn't need the distraction.'* She looked over at the woman again, who was putting a comforting hand on Lydia's arm. She saw Lydia tense slightly, but she didn't brush her away. Then the woman moved on, but first, behind Lydia's back, the woman caught Clark's eye and flashed a quick smile. It was not the smile of someone offering their sympathy. It was the smile of someone with a secret.

"I wonder how she knows them?" Dulcie said to Nick.

"Who?"

"The woman you were just talking to." She glanced at him briefly. He still looked annoyed. "Who is she?"

"Lexi," He said quickly. "Alexia Kent."

"She looks like someone who likes to manipulate people."

"You could say that." His clipped response told Dulcie to drop the subject.

Now Dulcie was somewhat annoyed. She had believed that she and Nick were working as a team. *'No, I'm just the person who got dragged into this,'* she thought. *'He does this for a living,'* she reminded herself. Still, she had thought they were getting to know each other more and that he might even be interested in her, in a somewhat non-professional way.

Maybe she was wrong on that score. Right now, she had to focus on the task at hand. Nick was watching Lydia closely. Dulcie whispered, "I saw Amelia Davenport-Jones in the kitchen. She asked why I was here."

"What did you say?"

"I told her I'd gone to high school with Jennifer and Lydia. It's true, but I don't think Amelia bought it. I mean, I think she knows there's another reason." She felt, rather than saw Nick nod. "I met her husband, too. Completely different. She clearly wears the pants in that relationship."

Nick smiled and Dulcie watched his face begin to relax. "Let's mingle," he said. "Try to speak as little as possible. Listen as much as you can."

"Yes, Detective," Dulcie quipped.

Nick smiled again. '*No,*' he thought. '*Stop. Don't fall for her. You can't.*' His lips stretched into a thin, straight line.

They drifted from one group to the next, saying whatever was appropriate, listening more. On the third or fourth group, one man was droning on about his boat and Dulcie became bored. She glanced out the window. It looked over a small section of the porch, only visible from where she stood, then to the beach. She stared at the beach until two people stepped onto the porch. It was Clark and the woman that had made Nick so tense, Lexi. Dulcie couldn't hear them but Lexi was clearly speaking smoothly to Clark, and he was growing more and more uncomfortable. She made one last comment that Dulcie thought might have been, "Think about it," and quickly left. Clark mopped his brow with his sleeve. Then he stumbled off the porch and walked out to the beach. He stood there for several minutes, then returned to the house.

Dulcie hadn't seen Lexi come back into the house. She quietly excused herself from the conversation and walked quickly to the back door. Peering out, she was just in time to see a red Mercedes pulling away. She thought it was Lexi at the wheel.

'*Interesting*,' she mused. She made her way back to the kitchen and poured more coffee. '*Time to talk with Lydia*,' she thought.

Lydia sat on one end of the couch looking exhausted. A couple stood over her, offering condolences as they were clearly heading for the door. Dulcie waited for them to go, then sat down next to Lydia.

"How are you holding up?" Dulcie said.

Lydia shook her head.

"How about we go outside and get some air. Want to sit on the porch?"

Dulcie gestured to the back door where fewer people would see them go. Lydia .looked at her gratefully and stood. Dulcie followed her out the door, around the corner of the house, and back up the porch steps. Dulcie quickly chose the wicker chair facing the porch door where any of the guests were likely to come out. Lydia sat in the other chair with her back to the door. The chair backs were high, so Lydia would not be easily seen. Lydia sank into the cushions and closed her eyes.

"This isn't me," she murmured. Dulcie said nothing. Lydia opened her eyes again. "You know who I am. Or who I was. I'm not used to this." Her eyes roamed the surroundings, taking in the exquisite little house, a few of the expensive cars parked nearby, the ocean in front of her. "My grandmother lives in a doublewide, for Chrissake!" She looked back at Dulcie. "I thought having money would be fun and would solve every problem. I do have nice clothes, a nice house, a nice car... but the price you pay for it.... That's what I never realized. These people," she glanced back into the house. "They have their own language and I don't understand it. They'll talk about a bottle of wine or a place that they've traveled to, and I know there's some underlying meaning, but I don't know what it is. It's like when you learn French in school, then go to Quebec. You understand the words people use, but you don't know what they mean."

She looked very small. *'She's in over her head,'* thought Dulcie.

"But Clark must help you. Doesn't he understand what you're going through?" Dulcie asked.

Lydia's face registered several emotions in rapid succession. She did not know what to do. She was caught. She had her plan, but it was all falling apart with Jennifer's death. Should she tell Dulcie? No, she couldn't. But she could at least tell her some things. Dulcie was practically a stranger now. It was so much easier to tell a stranger. She sat forward. "My husband doesn't have any understanding of people's feelings. Oh, he plays the part very, very well, certainly. But Clark thinks of Clark first. Always. He grew up with privilege. He was a little prince. Why wouldn't he think that way?"

"I'm sorry to hear that," said Dulcie, but Lydia didn't hear her. She'd made up her mind.

"You see, Clark has provided for me. He's given me a beautiful home, car, allowance... but I'm here on my own for days at a time. He likes to be in Boston. He has friends there. One in *particular*. He doesn't know that I know. I'd like to keep it that way."

Dulcie exhaled in a low whistle. She knew exactly what Lydia meant. "Why don't you divorce him?" she asked.

Lydia began playing with her rings. "I don't know. Because I feel stupid. Because I do like having the money. Because they'd all cackle about me and say how they knew I couldn't hack it. Because my own family, who thinks I'm stuck up now, would have a field day with it as well." And because she needed to figure out what to do about her plan.

"I know what you mean, I think," said Dulcie. "I inherited a lot of money recently, completely out of the blue. It changed my relationship with some people. In a couple of cases, we don't speak any more. I don't think I've changed really, but it's amazing what jealousy can do."

Lydia nodded. "Thank you. It helps to talk about it. I can't talk to anyone in Clark's circle, and I certainly can't tell anyone from my old group of friends or my family. I started to tell my Mom once, but she just got a little angry and said that I needed to *work on my marriage*."

Dulcie smiled ruefully. "I've never really understood what that means. But then, I've never been married."

"What it means is, *'Shut up, solve your own problems, and you better stay married or you'll have me to answer to.'* That's what it means." She closed her eyes again. "I just want to go as far away from here as I can get."

Dulcie reached over and squeezed Lydia's hand quickly. She stood and said, "You stay in that chair for a little while longer. No one's discovered you out here yet. Rest for a minute."

Lydia looked up at her. "Thank you," she said quietly.

"And Lydia, seriously, if you ever want to talk, I'm happy to. I mean that."

Lydia smiled softly and mouthed the word "thanks" as her eyes drifted closed.

Nobody wants to be the first guest to leave a social gathering, even if none of them want to be there in the first place. They all wait and watch to see if someone else will leave before them. Once that first brave soul goes, however, the floodgates open.

Dulcie watched people troop out the door one after another as though they were all late for somewhere else. If it had not been a funeral, she would have laughed. Lydia was discovered out on the porch shortly after Dulcie had left her, which was the perfect excuse for everyone. They could offer their final condolences and since they were already out the door and half way to their cars, they could just keep on walking. '*Why didn't I come out here sooner?* ' thought Lydia.

Locating Nick, Dulcie gave him a quick wave from across the room. He extricated himself and joined her. "Thought I'd lost you!" he said.

"No such luck," Dulcie replied. "I've had some interesting conversations, though. And have noticed a couple of things. Are you ready to go?"

"All too ready," he replied.

They slipped out the back door and trekked down the road to Nick's car. "I saw your friend leave. Rather quickly, I might add!"

Nick's easy saunter became a tight, measured stride. "Really."

"Yes. She'd been having a conversation with Clark Davenport-Jones that I would have to describe as clandestine. They were outside on the porch, down on the end where almost no one could see them. I was inside so I didn't hear anything, but he was clearly uncomfortable. At the end I could swear she said, '*Think about it.*' He literally mopped his brow and walked out to the beach for a few minutes. I went to the back door just in time to see her drive off. At least I think it was her. It was a red Mercedes sports car of some kind."

"That sounds about right," Nick said with a hint of sarcasm. "You didn't notice anything else? Did they exchange anything? Which one seemed in control?"

"They definitely didn't hand anything to each other. And I'd say that she was in control entirely. He looked surprised, confused, and maybe even a little scared. Doesn't that seem strange?"

"Yes. And no," said Nick. He didn't elaborate. "This is really helpful though. Anything else?"

"Yes. A good talk with Lydia. It seems she's pretty miserable in her marriage. She implied that Clark is cheating on her. She seems very lonely too. Her own family is jealous of her new status so she's essentially been ostracized, and she doesn't fit in with the wealthy set on Clark's side either."

The wealthy set. That had been Nick. The life had the illusion of freedom. You had the means to do whatever you liked, but it came with strings attached. Many, many strings. He knew what it was like. Whoever held the strings was in control of your life. He knew how it could smother you. "They'll eat her alive, if they haven't already," he said.

◌

Amelia Davenport-Jones was particularly silent on the drive back to Boston. She was usually barking some order at her husband or, at the very least, criticizing his driving. Ross was grateful for whatever was on her mind.

Amelia was reviewing the events of the afternoon and reflecting on her conversation, albeit brief, with Dulcie. She certainly had not expected to see her there. It threw Amelia off her game. *'I must set up lunch with her again,'* she thought. *'Soon. I don't want her changing her mind on that piece for sale. They've already pulled out of auction once.'* She yanked out her cell phone and scrolled through her contacts. Yes, there was Dulcie's number. She was sure she had entered it.

"Who are you calling?" said Ross. He wished he had not spoken as soon as the words left his mouth.

"No one!" Amelia spat out. "And watch out for that minivan. Damn things. People who buy those can't ever drive!"

'Here we go,' thought Ross.

Art is a lie that
makes us realize truth.
~ Pablo Picasso

CHAPTER ELEVEN

The differences between Dan Chambers and his sister Dulcie were many. The few traits that they did share were strong and defining. One was a love of the water. Any water. Another was dogged perseverance and a determination to get to the bottom of anything that puzzled them, big or small. If either latched on to a mystery, they could not stop thinking about it until they had some reasonable explanation. Otherwise, it bothered them continuously.

The lobster buoy that was out of place bothered Dan. It was only one, on its own, and clearly set wrong. Anyone else would have put it down quite simply to the work of an amateur. But that was not a good enough explanation for Dan. Something about it was strange.

The fact that Freddie had prattled on about it incessantly on the trip back certainly had not helped.

Obsessive by nature, Freddie had trouble letting things drop, too. He had even suggested that they go back out, after leaving off the passengers, to check on the buoy. Dan had laughed and explained the folly in that idea. The tide had already turned, quite literally. But he knew Freddie couldn't let it go, and neither could he.

ॐ

Dulcie stopped by Dan's boat the day after the funeral. One look at him told her that he was annoyed. "Okay, out with it. It can't be me because I just got here. What's up?"

Dan put down the chart he was analyzing. "It's nothing major. We got caught up on a buoy the other day. It took a few minutes to get free. Freddie was looking at it while we were untangling and noticed it was the only one around with that particular pattern of colors. I think it was set wrong too — it seemed to cross the other lines."

"So maybe it was an amateur? A recreational license? They don't know what they're doing sometimes."

"That's what I thought at first too, but something else is bothering me about it."

"You're obsessing, Dan."

"Yeah."

"But I know how you feel since I'm frequently guilty of that too." She looked down at the chart. "Where is it?"

Dan sat down and smoothed the chart out on the bench next to him. "Right here," he pointed.

Dulcie leaned over for a closer look and her sunglasses flipped off her head onto Dan's finger.

"Ow."

"Oops! Sorry." She retrieved them and looked again. Then she looked up at Dan. "Seriously?"

Dan's brow wrinkled. "What do you mean by that?"

Dulcie looked again. "Well, it just seems odd. That's the same cove where Jennifer Hully drowned. Or rather, that's the beach where they found her body. I don't think anyone knows exactly where she drowned." Dulcie pointed to the short span of beach on the chart.

They both sat silently for a few moments. "Should we go pull the trap?" asked Dulcie.

Dan laughed. "You know as well as I do that, not only is it illegal, but we could be staring down a shotgun if the owner shows up."

Dulcie nodded thoughtfully. "I know." She looked up at her brother. "However, I also know who we should tell about this." She pulled out her cell phone. "Dammit. Battery is dead. I forgot to plug it in last night."

Dan reached in his pocket for his phone and handed it to her. She looked at it curiously. Without her own list of contacts, Dulcie did not have the correct number. "How do I look up a number on this thing?"

Dan grabbed it back and rolled his eyes. "Whaddya need," he said without looking up.

"Nick," she said.

Dan grinned and raised his eyebrows.

Dulcie groaned. "You know what I mean! Just find the Portland Police Department number and I'll take it from there."

"Ummm hmmm!" Dan nodded, still grinning. He dialed the number and handed her the phone.

She pressed it to her ear just in time. "Yes, could I speak to Detective Nicholas Black, please?" She was silent for a few moments. "Yes, I'll leave a message." She heard his voice on the recorded message. He always sounded so clear and calm. Finally, she said, "Hi Nick, it's Dulcie." She elbowed Dan, who had just given her a mocking shove when she called him 'Nick.' "I just wanted to run something by you. If you get this in the next hour," she checked her watch, "by eleven o'clock, could you give me a call on Dan's phone? It's 555-2347." Dan shoved her again but this time shaking his head. "Oh, no wait, that's…," she watched Dan mouth the numbers, "Sorry, it's 2437. 555-2437. My battery is dead on my phone. Thanks, talk to you soon."

She clicked off the call and handed the phone back. "Thanks for your help, dork."

"Anytime." Dan's grin faded as he looked back at the chart. "Here's what I'm thinking. I'd like to go check out that buoy and the trap with it. How's your diving gear looking these days?"

"Actually, not bad. I just went last month. I'll have to get my tank filled." She looked back at the chart. "Bottom looks rough in places there. We should go at high tide, don't you think?"

Dan didn't even look. "Absolutely. Way easier."

They chatted for an hour, then Dulcie got up to leave. Dan's phone rang just as she stepped off the boat. He answered, then tossed it to her. She almost missed, nearly dropping it in the water. Dan just shook his head in dismay. Dulcie had never excelled at anything athletic.

"Hi, Nick? I've been talking to Dan. We want to run something by you. Are you nearby? We're on his boat... Great, I'll stay put and see you in a few."

Ten minutes later, Nicholas Black stood on the dock staring at the chart. "It's worth checking out. But Dulcie, you're not going alone. I'll go with you." He looked at Dan. "How soon can you get us out there?"

Dan said, "I've got two scheduled runs this afternoon. But I'd like to wait for high tide anyway. That's at five after six. I could meet you guys here at five o'clock. That'd give us plenty of time to get out there."

"And for me to fill my tank," said Dulcie.

"Me too," Nick added. "Great. Dulcie, why don't I grab your tank and get them both done."

"Perfect. It's back at the house."

"I'll give you a ride." He reached out for her hand and helped her off the boat. Dan smirked at Dulcie behind Nick's back.

"See you at five," she said sweetly to her brother, but gave him a deadly look.

⍥

Lydia had walked up and down the beach so many times, she was surprised that she had not scraped a channel through it. She didn't really care. Her sister was dead. Her marriage was a mess. She was a thief.

How had it all happened? Certainly not overnight. She had been flattered by Clark's interest. She tried not to take advantage of his money. From the start she wanted him to know that she liked *him*, not all of the things he could buy.

She kicked the sand. How could she be so naive? The engagement party was the first time she had noticed. He had told her that the statuesque blonde he had been talking with at length was an old girlfriend, nothing more. Did he think Lydia was stupid? Evidently, she actually was stupid. She trusted him. She wanted to believe him. Plus, she had been in the middle of planning what was rapidly becoming an expensive wedding. If that backfired, she would have felt like a complete idiot.

Instead, her marriage was now backfiring and she knew for certain that she was indeed a complete idiot. Yet she could not openly admit it. She could not accuse Clark. First, she had no real proof. Second, she had been stealing from his family.

The first theft was purely spite. She had always made a point of not taking money, not overspending. She wanted to show Clark's parents that she wasn't a gold digger. When she realized that he was cheating on her, however, she wanted some kind of revenge. The best revenge she could think of was to take something from them. She had been alone for several moments in the attic of her in-laws' Beacon Hill townhouse. The painting was quite small, and had a pocket attached to the back with plenty of documentation. Glancing through the papers, she saw that Amelia Davenport-Jones had bought it several years before for slightly more than fifteen thousand. Small change in their world.

Lydia would never forget how it dug into her skin when she stuffed the corner of it in the waistband of her jeans. She was wearing a loose, bulky sweater. Quietly she had gone down the stairs and managed to transfer it into her tote bag without being seen. Joining the family in the library for drinks, she had nearly jumped when Amelia asked, "Did you find what you were looking for?" Lydia had forgotten that she had originally gone to the attic to find a lamp that Clark thought he remembered.

Jennifer had given her the idea of selling the painting. Jennifer was her confidant for everything. Jennifer knew about Clark and his affair. She agreed to hide the painting for Lydia, and then helped her to find a buyer for it. They split the eighteen thousand dollars.

Afterward, Jennifer had volunteered to spy on Clark, but Lydia stopped her. Even though she knew he was cheating, she didn't want proof. Yes, it would show that she was right, but it would also prove what a fool she was.

No, she would bide her time. She would steal and sell and raise enough money to break away from him on her own terms. Then she could divorce him without anyone knowing about his infidelity and without suing for any extra money. She would keep her pride, her mother-in-law would having nothing to say, and she would be self-reliant.

What now, though? Jennifer still had two works that Lydia had taken. She didn't know where they were, and that frightened her. If they were found with Jennifer's things, they would be identified. That could lead directly back to Lydia.

She was also concerned by the way Jennifer had died. It simply wasn't like her to dive alone. Lydia instinctively knew that Jennifer had not.

Something told Lydia that she was in danger. She looked up at her beachfront cottage. Clark stood in the window, staring out at her. He quickly moved back into the shadows.

It's not what you look at that matters,
it's what you see.
~ Henry David Thoreau

CHAPTER TWELVE

The last of Dan's passengers stepped off the boat as Dulcie came walking down the pier. She had her diving gear in a big canvas bag strapped to a luggage carrier. Navigating it down the bumpy timbers was not an easy chore and Dan laughed when she nearly dumped it over.

"You know, you'd burn off a few more calories if you carried that," he said.

She looked up at him. "It's too much to carry in one trip."

"Ever heard of making two? That's even more calories." He grinned.

"Shut up and help me with this."

They had just loaded everything when Nick arrived. "See," said Dan. "He's carrying his gear. No roller carts for him!"

Nick looked from Dulcie to Dan quizzically.

Dulcie heaved a sigh. "You see, Nick. Dan just made fun of me because I didn't carry my gear, I rolled it down the dock with this." She pointed to the luggage carrier.

Nick glanced at it, then looked at her. Then he looked at Dan. "Well, she is only about a hundred pounds soaking wet."

Dan burst out laughing and said, "Whoa! She's a lot more than that! She's actually...OUCH!" Dulcie's sharp elbow jabbed into his side.

Freddie jumped down from the bridge. "You gonna need me?"

Dan nodded. "Wouldn't hurt. They'll be in the water," he said pointing to the other two, "so it'd be good to have someone watching for them and someone else watching the boat. Can you stay?"

"Lemme call the missus." He pulled out a very old cell phone and went back up on the bridge.

"And we can guess how that call will go," said Dan. "Honey, can I go out on one more run or do you need me back at the house?" Then Dan's voice went up an octave. "Ohhh, nooo, Fred! You do whatever they need on that boat! You stay out all night if they need you! I'm just going to the mall with MaryAnn. Have fun dear!" He stopped when he heard Freddie clamoring down again.

"Yup, no problem. She's going to the mall with her friend so I'd be home alone anyway," Freddie said.

Nick turned away to hide his smile. He looked over at Dulcie who was suddenly very busy pulling her gear out of her bag.

"Right then! Freddie, get ready to cast off the lines. We're off to Kettle Cove!" Dan vaulted back up to the bridge and started the engine.

Dulcie and Nick watched the coastline slip by as they made their way out of the harbor. "I have to remind myself that people pay thousands to come up here in the summer," said Nick. They rounded Portland Head Light, one of the most famous lighthouses in the world.

"I know!" said Dulcie. "Hard not to be jaded. I try to tell myself often that I'm pretty lucky."

The ocean swells were low and steady, and the boat travelled easily across them as it rounded the cape and reached Kettle Cove. Dulcie hauled her wetsuit out of her bag and laid it out on the deck. Then, in one quick motion, she stripped off the T-shirt dress that she was wearing. Nick heard himself gasp and tried to stop. She had on a bathing suit of course. A simple, one-piece, bright blue suit. He hoped she hadn't heard him.

Nick forced himself to focus on his own gear but stole glances at her as she pulled on her wetsuit. Her legs were tanned, but not overly so. Just a soft, warm color. He could see the muscles in her legs and arms as she worked the wetsuit over them. Not too much muscle, just enough. He tried not to think about her hips. They rounded perfectly to a small waist. He took a deep breath and yanked on his own wetsuit.

"Got it! Right ov-ah heya!" For some reason, Freddie's accent was thicker when he yelled. He had spotted the buoy. Dan slowed the engine and they gently drifted toward it.

"I'm not going to anchor right on top of it," he said. "I'll drop it a few yards away. That'll give you guys some room."

Nick and Dulcie nodded. The early evening sun was shining at an angle into the water, and they could see the rope from the buoy descend downward. Dulcie hoisted her tank into her buoyancy vest resting on the bench, and snapped it in place. Then she sat down in front of the vest, reached back and pulled it forward. This was the part she never liked. The gear was heavy and difficult to get on. Once it was on, it was even harder to move around the boat. She grabbed her mask beside her and pulled it onto her forehead, leaving her eyes uncovered for the moment.

"All set?" asked Nick who had just done exactly the same thing beside her.

Dulcie nodded. Then she grabbed his arm. "I want to try something down there. You said that Jennifer was drugged. I want to see if I can still breathe if I'm not paying attention to the fact that I'm diving."

"Uh, I'm not sure if I like this idea," Nick said.

"It'll be fine. If I lose the regulator just hand it back to me. When I'm going to try it, I'll do this," She waved her hand back and forth in a horizontal line in front of her. "Then just watch me and see what happens."

"And if I say 'No'?"

"She'll do it anyway," said Dan. He had just joined them.

"Correct," Dulcie laughed.

Nick and Dulcie both tested their air, and then pulled down their masks. They waddled to the stern and, steadying each other, pulled on flippers. Nick stepped off first, making a big splash as he bounced into the water. Once in, he turned quickly to watch Dulcie.

Reminding herself to breathe normally, she made the giant step off the stern. She plunged into the water, watching it engulf her. She shivered as it quickly seeped beneath her wetsuit. That was the part she disliked the most. Maine ocean water was never warm, and today was no exception. It always took a few minutes for her body to heat it under the neoprene and for the wetsuit to do its job.

She looked over at Nick and gave him the OK sign. He returned it. Then he flashed a thumbs down sign. Dulcie always thought it was funny that for divers, this was a good thing. It meant that they were ready to descend. She returned the sign and slowly they made their way down, following the rope attached to the oddly colored buoy.

The wooden lobster trap at the bottom was beneath only twenty-five feet of water, even at high tide. Dulcie and Nick poked at it gently. There were no lobsters in it. Dulcie looked more closely. She noticed that part of it had been altered so that lobsters would not be able to make their way in. She pointed to the rigged piece that she saw, but wasn't sure if Nick understood.

Nick began to gently shift the trap. At first Dulcie was not certain what he was doing, but then realized that he wanted to look under it while disturbing the bottom as little as possible. They were already kicking up silt and debris, and the visibility was becoming poorer. She helped him to pry the trap up slowly.

Nick located his flashlight and skimmed the strong beam over the sand. Nothing unusual. He motioned for Dulcie to hold the trap up at an angle. Nick gently worked his hands into the sand underneath. He moved his way along carefully while Dulcie was beginning to wonder if this was a worthless outing after all. Suddenly, Nick stopped and quickly looked up at her. His eyes were very big. Gradually, and with deliberate care, he pulled out a long, black plastic tube with a weight on one end.

Dulcie forgot what she was doing and let the trap fall. Clouds of silt billowed into the water. She lost sight of Nick for a moment. When she saw him again, he was giving her the thumbs up signal. He wanted to ascend. It had taken Dulcie months to stop using that as the 'I'm OK' sign when she had first learned to dive. She shook her head and waved her arm in front of her horizontally as she had on the boat. She wanted to try her experiment.

She saw bubbles stream from Nick's mouthpiece and knew he had just exhaled loudly. He was not happy with this, but made the OK sign.

Dulcie willed her entire body to become limp. She relaxed all of the muscles in her mouth. Then she closed her eyes. She was floating, dreaming, sleeping. Her breath barely registered. As she relaxed she couldn't feel the weight of the vest or even her wetsuit against her. She was drifting in time. She thought that this was what it must feel like to be in outer space. As her body slipped through the water, rolling with the slight motion of the tide's current, her breathing stayed steady. The mouthpiece stayed in.

She wanted to continue like this, floating, drifting... Suddenly a huge force grabbed her arm and yanked her sideways. She opened her eyes half frightened and saw Nick's eyes directly in front of hers, their masks nearly touching. He looked angry. She was breathing hard now, bubbles streaming out each time she exhaled. He pushed her away to arms length and, without letting go, gave her the OK sign. She returned it. Then he jerked the thumbs up sign at her and without waiting for a reply slowly ascended. He never let go of her arm.

When they reached the surface, Nick motioned to the boat. Dulcie pulled out her mouthpiece and started to speak, but Nick yanked out his own from his mouth and cut her off. "Not now. Keep breathing your air. Get back on the boat, then we'll talk."

Puzzled and somewhat annoyed, she replaced her mouthpiece. Nick followed her back to where Dan was waiting for them at the stern.

When she reached him Dulcie took off her fins and handed them up, then climbed the ladder and eased herself down to sit on the bench. She unbuckled her vest, pretending not to notice Nick pulling himself up onto the boat. He sat opposite her. Dan took their tanks out of their vests and stowed them where they would not roll around, then threw Dulcie a towel. "I'll pull the anchor up and get Freddie started on heading us back." One look at them told him to leave them alone for a few moments.

Dulcie stood and unzipped the back of her wetsuit. She sat down again to peel off the top part. She waited for Nick to speak first.

Grabbing the towel he scrubbed his hair dry then turned his full attention to her. "What the hell was that?" he said quietly.

His voice made Dulcie nervous. "What?" she asked.

"You know what. I tried to get your attention three times! I grabbed your fin, your leg, your arm... I thought something was really wrong, that you were holding your breath and had an embolism or…"

Dulcie stared at him. "But I told you I was going to…"

"You didn't tell me you were going to play dead!" He slid over on the bench beside her. "Dulcie, if anything had happened, I don't know what I would have, I mean, I was… worried." Without thinking he put his hand on her cheek, turning her face toward his. "I thought something had happened," he whispered.

Dulcie stared into his very gray eyes. Her heart was pounding. She put her hand on his, still touching her face.

"All set to head back! Anyone need a beer?" Dan's voice boomed from the bridge.

Nick quickly slid away from Dulcie and busied himself with pulling off his wetsuit. Dulcie looked at him, then toward the bridge. She couldn't see Dan in the shadows, but knew he could see her. "Yes, please! Two!" She didn't clarify that both could easily be for her.

With the boat underway, Dan came to the stern carrying three bottles of beer. He handed one to each of them. "So what'd you discover? Anything good?"

Dulcie had forgotten about Nick's find. She turned quickly to him. "What the heck is that tube, and what's in it?" she said excitedly.

Dan's eyes were wide as Nick pulled the tube out of the straps on his buoyancy vest. "Where was that?" he asked

"Under the lobster trap. Buried just enough so no one could actually see it, and weighted so it'd stay down." He slid the towel along it, drying it thoroughly, then handed the tube to Dulcie. "Want to do the honors?"

She made sure her own hands were dry, then took it.

"Wait, what if it's a bomb?" she said nervously.

Nick snorted. "It's not a bomb."

"How do you know?" Dulcie demanded.

Nick leaned back against the cushion behind him. "First of all, it's way too light. Secondly, the way it was hidden, it doesn't fit the profile of a bomb."

"You're sure?" said Dulcie holding it gingerly.

"If I wasn't, would I have given it to you?"

"Good point," Dulcie replied. Carefully opening the cover, she peered inside. "Can I have your flashlight?" she asked Nick. He pulled it off his vest and wiped it dry before handing it to her. She shined the strong beam into the tube, and nearly smacked heads with Dan who tried to look in at the same time. "Would you mind?" she said without looking up.

Dulcie slipped her fingers in and gently pulled out what looked like two large pieces of paper, each encased in clear plastic. She unrolled them and let out a low whistle.

"What have we got?" said Nick.

"We'll have to get them authenticated for sure, but this one," she held up the larger of the two, "looks like a Jean Cocteau."

"Looks like a poster to me," laughed Dan.

"And it is!" replied Dulcie. "A poster worth about ten grand, give or take, if I'm not mistaken." She held up the smaller piece. "This, on the other hand, is an original. I think it's a Calder."

"Didn't he do sculptures?" asked Nick.

"Those hanging ones! Mobiles!" added Dan. "See Dulcie, I've listened all those times you've tried to educate me."

"You're both right," Dulcie said. "He actually did a little of everything. BMW even commissioned him to paint a car."

"So what's this one worth?" asked Nick.

"It's hard for me to say, but I'd bet at least two or three times what the Cocteau would get."

They sat silently, staring at the two artworks that Dulcie was holding. Dan took a long swig of his beer, then said, "So you're telling me that about forty thousand dollars was sitting down there on the bottom of the ocean?"

"Buried under a lobster trap," added Dulcie.

Nick looked at her. It was too much of a coincidence. "Jennifer did this. She must have. But where did they come from? How did she get them? And was she just the middle-man in the game?"

"Isn't it always the middle-man who gets killed first? They know too much," said Dan while shaking his head.

"True. On TV, anyway." Nick was thoughtful. He reached over and took the Calder, examining it closely. "Do you think these are the real thing?"

"My bet is *yes, for sure,* since she went to great lengths to hide them."

"How could she sell them, though? Is the black market that strong?"

Dulcie's smile was rueful. "Unfortunately, it is. Especially for things like this that aren't the top-tier works. If you tried to sell a Calder sculpture on the black market, that would be a lot more difficult, but a work on paper like this," she took the drawing back from Nick, "would be much easier. Less demand. Fewer people even know that he did these."

"And what about the poster?" Dan added.

"Same thing, more or less. This would have had multiple copies printed, so it isn't an original work. It's valuable now because few remain and because it's a Cocteau. But like Calder, he was multifaceted too. He was best known for his writing." Dulcie took the Cocteau piece and carefully rolled it back up with the Calder work. "We'd better get these out of the light." She slid them back into the tube.

Nick stared across the water at the shoreline rushing by. "The Feds will be all over this once they hear about it. They took the other painting as soon as I put it in my report."

Dulcie looked at him closely. "So, does that mean that we never saw these?" she asked. "For now, anyway?"

"Yeah, that's what I'm thinking. I just need more time to put this together."

Dan's eyes swiveled back and forth between them. "I didn't see a thing! In fact, I think I'll just mosey on back to my fridge and see if I can scare up another round here for us. They are light beers after all, right? So two equals one?" He chuckled at his own joke as he made his way into the comparative darkness of the cabin.

Dulcie's doorbell rang an hour later. She had showered and changed into a light cotton dress. The evening was hot and a bit sticky but she had hesitated to turn on the air conditioning. She needed the fresh air, however uncomfortable it might be.

She had turned on a fan, however, and almost tripped over the cord as she hurried to the door. She peeked through the window beside it. Nick stood on the step with a large paper bag. Dulcie opened the door quickly. "Chicken fried rice," he said. "And a few extra things too."

Dulcie laughed. "Looks like you ordered the whole menu! Good. I'm starving." Grabbing the bag, she motioned for him to come in. She put the bag on the kitchen table and tore it open, all in one motion. Nick looked at her with surprise. "Oh," she said, somewhat embarrassed. "I've discovered it's the easiest way to get everything out. They pack it pretty tightly."

"The quickest way, too!" added Nick.

"You must think I'm a glutton," she said as she opened the refrigerator.

"Actually, I don't. To be honest, it annoys me when women, and it's usually women but sometimes men, eat like birds. It makes me nervous. If they control that much in their lives, what else are they holding back?"

"I never thought of it that way, but it makes sense." Dulcie pointed to a drawer where Nick found silverware. She poured two glasses of wine. Just a simple merlot, nothing fancy. She didn't want to intimidate Nick, although she had forgotten that he was the one brought up with privilege. "So what's the next step?" she asked as they both ate out of the white cardboard boxes.

Having quickly finished his first box, Nick reached for another. He pried it open, peered in at the contents and smiled. Dulcie laughed.

"I think the next step is to have another talk with our grieving sister Lydia." He dug in to something with noodles. "What are your thoughts on her?"

"Probably the same as yours. She hasn't been telling us everything. Not even close, I don't think."

"Here's a crazy thought: what if she killed her sister?"

Dulcie paused for a moment, slowly sipping her wine. She shook her head and swallowed. "I don't think so. Both times I've talked to her she's seemed genuinely upset. But you know, Nick, she also seemed a little frightened. Did you get that from her?"

"I did, but that's often the reaction when someone is killed."

"Maybe, but she doesn't know that her sister was killed. So far, she just knows that it was an accident."

"True. I think she suspects, though. She was adamant about Jennifer not diving alone."

"Could she be saying that just to point the finger at someone else?" Dulcie asked.

"It's possible."

"Is that lo mein?" Dulcie asked, pointing at a partially open box. Nick nodded and handed it to her. She popped it open and stuck her chopsticks in. "What can I do to help?"

"I've been thinking. Is there any way you could track down the ownership of those two items we found today? And could you do it without anyone knowing?"

"I can certainly try. If they were sold recently, there would be a record. Especially if they were at auction."

"What if they weren't sold recently?"

"That makes it more difficult, but I can still look back through records. I'll also see if there are any collectors of either artist in the area. I'm assuming that whoever they were stolen from would be somewhat local."

"I think that's a good assumption. How quickly can you find out?"

"I'll start online tonight. I can make some calls from the office tomorrow morning. I can't make any promises."

"No, of course not."

"So other than talking to Lydia, what are you doing next?" Dulcie asked.

"I think it's time to make a statement that we suspect foul play, then bring everyone in for questioning. The first thing I need to do is establish where family members and close friends were on the night Jennifer was killed. Someone put poison on her equipment, and they had to do it just before she went on that dive."

"I wonder where they got the drug?" Dulcie mused.

"Good question. Could have been bought illegally, stolen from a pharmacy, or even taken from a vet. I know they use it for animals, too."

Dulcie put her glass down hard, then cringed thinking that she'd broken it. Nick looked startled.

"Sorry. But I just remembered. The other day I found out that Lydia's new father-in-law takes care of horses. He's an equine vet."

Nick's eyes narrowed. "I thought none of them had to work. The Davenport-Joneses have tons of money."

"They don't have to work. But Ross Davenport-Jones evidently wanted to be a veterinarian. He's the youngest of a bunch of brothers. I heard that he was always the quiet one and wanted to go his own way."

Nick sat back in his chair. He knew all about that – going one's own way. He suddenly felt sympathetic toward Ross Davenport-Jones.

Dulcie was still talking. "I wonder how he ended up with Amelia, though? That seems like such a mismatch."

"Didn't have much of a choice," Nick mumbled.

"Sorry?" said Dulcie. "What did you say?"

"I was just thinking out loud. Kind of." He began gathering up the empty boxes.

"No, no! You made dinner, I'll do the dishes!" Dulcie took the boxes from him and threw them in the trash. They both laughed. Dulcie realized how much she liked Nick's smile. He had a dimple on one side, and she suddenly understood that it had far too much potential to make her melt.

"I'll get going. Are you sure you're comfortable having those pieces of art here?" Nick asked.

"Yes, absolutely. This place," she gestured around her, "has extra insurance for works that I have here temporarily. It isn't uncommon for me to have a lesser-valued piece with me."

"Lesser-valued," repeated Nick. "It's all relative, isn't it."

Dulcie smiled. "Yes, I'm afraid it is. I'll call you tomorrow if I find out anything."

"Same here. And Dulcie," he had just pulled open the heavy wooden door and stopped in the open doorway. Dulcie could feel a cool ocean breeze coming through. "I'm sorry about earlier, on the dive, and after. I was concerned and...."

"No worries," she said softly. "'Night, Nick."

He reached up as if to touch her cheek again, as he had on the boat, but drew his hand away. "G'night," he said quickly and left.

Dulcie closed the door gently and took a deep breath from behind it. Well! Working with Detective Nicholas Black was certainly getting interesting! She cleaned up the rest of the Chinese food boxes and wiped off the kitchen table. Pouring a second glass of merlot she slipped off her shoes by the front door, then went in the next room to her desk. She carefully put the wine on another table. She had already ruined one laptop with a particularly expensive, and not to mention excellent, cabernet. It was not going to happen again.

Three hours later she yawned, stretched, and closed the computer. She'd made very little progress. The research confirmed that her guesses had been correct on the value of each work. However, she had not been successful finding either of them in recent lists of sales.

"I'll have to start again tomorrow. And talk with some people. Maybe that will point me in a different direction." She went to the kitchen and rinsed out the glass. Then she unlocked the safe that she'd had installed in the back of her clothes closet, secured the artworks in it, and went to bed.

The object isn't to make art,
it's to be in that wonderful state
which makes art inevitable.
~ Robert Henri

CHAPTER THIRTEEN

The BMW convertible hugged the curves of the winding road. Clark's baseball cap nearly flew off as a gust came in from the ocean. He knew he was driving too fast. He didn't care.

Clark was in over his head. Lexi had called him that morning. In her ever-so-subtle way, she demanded that he spend the weekend with her. She said that she was lonely. He knew that she was simply bored. He tried to refuse, but her next statement made him nearly drop the phone. "I know about you and Jennifer."

How could she know? *What* could she know? It wasn't like they'd done anything, really. He had met Jennifer for drinks a couple of times, just to get to know her better, he said. The second time he'd had a few too many and made a pass at her. She didn't brush him off. He was surprised at that. They went back to his boat that night but he'd been drunk and couldn't...

couldn't. Not for lack of trying, either. It was before the wedding, so he didn't think it counted as officially fooling around.

He knew Lydia would not see it that way, especially now that Jennifer was dead. But how could Lexi know? Maybe she was just guessing. Maybe it was all a bluff. He couldn't take the chance, though.

Clark pulled the car into a scenic overlook and stopped. He got out and sat on the hood, looking across the ocean. He had two choices: come clean with Lydia about Lexi and Jennifer, or lie to her about the weekend and continue the charade. Clark was not a strong man. The second option seemed much simpler. Plus, it had the bonus of Lexi, at night....

He found himself smiling, and simultaneously hated himself for it. He loved Lydia. Really he did. But maybe he just wasn't cut out to be a husband? He was glad that Jennifer was gone and he didn't have to worry about that angle any more. Just as long as Lexi kept quiet.

ɞ

Lydia heard a knock at the door and instantly froze. She did not like unannounced visitors. She peeked through the window overlooking the driveway and saw Nicholas Black's car parked there. "Dammit!" she said softly. She heard the knock again.

Pulling herself up to be as tall as possible, which did not accomplish much, she went over to the door and opened it quickly. "Detective Black? Hello! I thought I heard the door. I was out on the front porch."

Nick knew a lie when he heard one, but he let it pass. "Then shall we go back out? If you have a moment, I'd like to ask you a few more questions."

"Yes, of course," she motioned toward the porch and followed him out. She sank into the cushions of a wicker chair. Nick sat on the edge of the one opposite. "Can I get you something to drink?" Lydia asked, almost lazily.

Nick shook his head. "No, thank you. I won't be long. I just wanted to let you know before it becomes public. Your sister did not drown in an accident. We believe that she was murdered."

Lydia's entire body shot forward in the chair, as though an electric current had just run through it. "WHAT!?"

"We found traces of a drug called ketamine on the mouthpiece of her diving equipment and in her body. Do you know if she used drugs recreationally?"

Lydia's head shook back and forth emphatically, her dark hair swinging out to the sides. "No! *Never*! I've told you that she liked taking risks but she wasn't stupid. She also hated to lose control of anything, especially herself. She didn't even drink very much for that reason." Lydia's body began to shake. "You can't be right, though. No one would want to kill her!"

Nick looked out at the ocean and took a deep breath, hoping that Lydia would do the same. He had been trained in all types of interrogation. For this kind, informal and subtle, he knew he wanted her to mirror him. He watched as Lydia looked out across the water and took a deep breath too. Her shaking subsided.

"We believe that she was involved in the theft of artworks. Lydia, what I'm about to tell you was not made public, and for the moment we need to keep it that way." She nodded in response. "When your sister was found, she had with her a watertight tube that contained a rolled-up van Gogh painting. As you can imagine, it's very valuable. We've just found two more similar items," he hesitated, not sure whether to tell her where they had been hidden, "that had most certainly been in her possession, but did not belong to her."

Lydia's head was spinning. *Stay calm*, she willed herself. *What would Jennifer do in this situation?* She looked up at the detective wide-eyed. "A van Gogh? What were the other two?"

Odd question. Why would she care what they were? Nick locked that back in his memory to consider later. "A Jean Cocteau poster and an Alexander Calder sketch."

"Are those valuable too?" she appeared very innocent.

"Yes. Not as much as the van Gogh, obviously, but still worth quite a lot. Do you know anything about art, Mrs. Davenport-Jones?"

The formal name threw Lydia off her guard. "Don't call me that!" she snapped. "I mean, please just call me Lydia. I mean...," she sat back in the chair and began to cry.

Nick sighed. Now he would get nowhere. "I'm sorry to upset you. Can you tell me if you were aware of your sister's interest in art?"

Lydia sniffed loudly. "I knew she liked it. She liked going to museums. I know she went to some gallery openings, too. But I never thought...."

Nick took out a handkerchief and handed it to her. He never actually used one himself. It was only in his pocket for occasions like this. They were almost never returned so he found himself handing out brand new ones nearly every time. He'd gone through boxes of them. She thanked him and snuffled into it.

"Lydia, I have to ask everyone this question so please don't take offense. Can you tell me your exact whereabouts on the afternoon and evening before Lydia was found? That would be last Monday."

"Let me think," she looked up at him through tear filled eyes. "We had been at Clark's parent's house in Boston for the weekend. We stayed over on Sunday night and decided to drive up late in the morning on Monday. We got back here around one o'clock, I think. Yes, near one. We had a late lunch when we got here. Then I just puttered around for the afternoon and took a long walk on the beach. Clark and I had dinner here that night."

"Can anyone vouch for you other than Clark?"

"One of our neighbors may have seen the car. And someone may have seen me walking on the beach. Oh, and we ordered pizza so the delivery guy could tell you that we were home."

"That sounds fine. Thanks for being honest with me. I'm sorry to have to ask these questions, but can you think of anyone who would want to kill your sister, for any reason?"

Lydia eyes were red now and beginning to swell. "No. We weren't very close, but... No." Tears streamed down her face again. Lydia heard a car pull into the driveway. "Oh god, who is that?"

Nick stood up and craned his neck. "It's just your husband. I'm going to have a word with him, then I'll send him out here if that's all right with you?"

Lydia nodded without looking up.

Nick quickly rounded the porch and caught a surprised looking Clark Davenport-Jones getting out of his shiny BMW. "Everything all right?" he asked.

Nick looked at him squarely. "No, I'm afraid not. I've just been speaking with your wife and I'm sorry to say that she's quite upset."

"What the hell do you think...?"

Nick put up his hand, stopping Clark before he could finish. He quickly added, "I had to tell her before she saw it publicly announced. Her sister's death was not accidental. She was murdered."

Nick watched carefully. Clark took off his cap, rubbed his hand through his hair several times, then put the cap back on. "Can you give me any details?"

"Yes, but first I need to know where you were last Monday afternoon and evening," Nick said.

"Wait a second! You don't think that I...!"

"It's just routine."

Clark looked at the ground. "Let's see. Monday. We came back from my parents place. In Boston. Had some lunch. Lydia went for a walk. I went for a drive. We got pizza for supper. That's all I really remember at this point. Now can you tell me how she was killed? I thought she ran out of air."

"Yes, she did. But she was drugged with a substance called ketamine. Have you ever heard of it?"

"As a matter of fact, I have. My dad uses it sometimes with the horses. I remember seeing it in his office medicine cabinet."

"Does he have a lock on the cabinet?"

"Yes, of course he does."

"Do you have any interest in art, Mr. Davenport-Jones?"

Clark snorted. "Art? No. None. My mother's crazy about it. Bores the hell out of me. She insisted I take an art history class in college. Failed it. All I know is that it fills up space on the walls and that's all I really care about."

"Do you know why anyone would want to kill your wife's sister?"

The image of Jennifer on the boat with him flashed into his mind. She had laughed when he couldn't perform. He had wanted to kill her then.

"No, I have no idea. I didn't really know her at all. Detective, are we done? I think I need to be with my wife right now." He moved toward the house.

"Of course. I'll be in touch," Nick replied.

'*I'm sure you will,*' thought Clark.

ᛉ

Dulcie swiveled back and forth in her office chair scrolling through the contact list on her phone. She had just spoken with curators at three different museums asking them about recent sales they may have heard about, along with who collected Cocteau, Calder, or anything even similar. She had tried to sound very casual, as though she were testing the waters for a new exhibit. So far, she had drawn a blank.

She decided to switch course and contact a gallery owner in Boston who specialized in graphic art pieces and promotional posters. She had not spoken with him in quite some time, so a call out of the blue would not be unusual. She hoped that it would simply sound like she was getting in touch for a collegial chat.

The phone rang several times before she heard, "Zee Gallerie Comedie et Tragadie! How can I be of service?"

"Jean Louis, so good to hear you! It's Dulcie Chambers. How have you been?"

"Dulciieee! My sweet petit! Your voice, it makes me smile! And god knows, your poor Jean Louis, he has had little to smile of recently."

Dulcie laughed. She knew otherwise. Jean Louis had just sold a rare work for slightly under one hundred thousand dollars. It had been in all the papers. "Yes, Jean Louis. You've had a hard time of it, I know." She heard his low chuckle. "I just wanted to congratulate you, first of all. What a find, and what a sale!"

"Ah, oui. Your poor friend Jean Louis, he has the luck for one time. I will not have to close the shop, at least for a leeeetle while now."

Dulcie could tell from his voice that he was smiling broadly. She smiled too. Jean Louis could plead poverty, but he was an extremely savvy businessman. "That's so good to hear, Jean Louis."

"Oui, oui! So my dear Dulcieee, what can I do for you?"

'*And there's the businessman coming through*,' thought Dulcie. Get the happy small-talk over with quickly, move on to the real subject, and then close the deal. She liked him for that. "I'm cooking up some ideas for a new exhibit. Something a little different. We've had the usual run of seascapes and Homers and such up here. Recently I've been thinking about travel and event posters."

"Right up my alleeeey, my Dulciee!"

"Very much so. You were the first person that I thought of. Would you know of some private collectors who might be willing to loan some pieces? Has anyone bought items from you that are particularly notable in the past several years?" Dulcie held her breath hoping the last bit wasn't too obvious.

"Hmmm. As you know, zee sales, they must remain *confidentiel* of course, but I can tell you who I have seen in my small shop, *certainement!* Let me think..."

Dulcie heard tapping on the keyboard of a computer. "Mais oui! There is Emile Lawson, Stephen Baker, Amelia Davenport-Jones, Carter..."

Dulcie cut him off, "Who was that last one? Amelia Davenport-Jones?"

"Oui! Yes! She collects many things. She is, what is the word? *Insatiable!*"

Dulcie laughed. "I think that's the same in English, Jean Louis. I'm sorry to interrupt. I had lunch with her the other day and had no idea. Go on, please." Dulcie heard none of the remainder of Jean Louis's list. He finished, and she politely thanked him, then pretended someone had come into her office so she could quickly say goodbye.

She put down the phone and leaned back in her chair, then spun around several times. Certainly a coincidence that the Davenport-Jones name would crop up. She was a collector after all. It really could not be that relevant, could it?

Perhaps another lunch with Amelia was in order. '*No,*' thought Dulcie, '*I can't stand an entire lunch. Maybe I'll just meet her for a drink.*' She looked up the number and dialed.

℘

Ross Davenport-Jones had no idea what to do about the horse. He also had no idea what to do about the situation with Jennifer. Should he come clean? Should he walk away? He was driving up the winding dirt road toward Winterhaven Stables. The goldenrod grew in large patches all around. Ross sneezed hard, twice, almost turning the car into the ditch the second time. He pulled over and stopped, fishing out a handkerchief.

Lexi Kent was trotting up the road but slowed her horse when she saw the car. She knew who Ross was now. She stopped Hadrian, who kicked at the pebbles beneath him. "Are you all right?" she asked Ross.

He looked up, startled. He hadn't heard her while honking into the handkerchief loudly to clear his nose. "Yes, yes. Damned goldenrod!"

"There does seem to be quite a lot of it this year. It's very pretty, actually."

"Unless you're allergic to it," Ross groused. He shoved the handkerchief back into his pocket.

"Are you coming to check on one of the horses? I think you were with Attagirl last time I saw you here. Is she doing any better?"

Ross started the car to cover his unease. "I have to check on several, actually." He looked up at her. "Do you ride here often? I haven't seen you around very much."

Lexi laughed. "Yes, considering that Donald Winters is my uncle." She could have sworn Ross looked startled. "He bought me this horse," she patted Hadrian's neck, "for my birthday this summer. I love to ride. I'm around quite a bit now." She cocked her head sideways, looking at him. "Didn't I see you at the funeral for that poor girl who drowned? What was her name... Jennifer Hully?"

Ross had seen Lexi there and had taken pains to avoid being seen by her. Evidently he had not been successful. "Um, yes. A tragedy," he muttered.

"Did you know her well?"

It was an innocent enough question. He stared at her for a moment. "Her sister is married to my son," he said simply.

"Ah, yes. That's right. Clark Davenport-Jones. I know Clark from college. I was in the area when I heard about the accident, so thought it would only be right to offer my sympathies." She smiled warmly at Ross.

"That was kind of you," he muttered. Why was it that he didn't believe her?

Hadrian tossed his head and pulled on the reins. Lexi giggled. "It looks like I must be off now. Hadrian's really been needing some exercise. Good to see you again." She kicked her heels into Hadrian's sides and set off on a quick trot.

Ross eased the car back onto the road and drove slowly. Now he knew that she had seen him in Attagirl's stable. She had probably guessed every detail of his plan. She had come to Jennifer's funeral services just to torment him. Why? What did she want?

ೞ

Portland's waterfront restaurants vied for both local and tourist dollars. The establishments were in abundance along the narrow streets of Portland's busy Old Port section. The tourist literature liked to refer to it as quaint or cozy. '*Without the crowds, it would be,*' thought Dulcie as she sat at the bar of one of her favorites, an upscale Irish pub. Someone bumped her arm as they squeezed by her. She nearly spilled pinot noir down the front of her dress. '*This is why I wear dark colors,*' she thought.

Dulcie loved Maine summers, but they had always involved the beach and boats and the water. Portland was certainly very nice during the summer, but by August she found herself yearning for January when everyone was gone.

"Ah, there you are." Amelia Davenport-Jones's flat voice grated on Dulcie's ears. The older woman plunked herself down on the barstool next to Dulcie. "And you have a drink. Good. I like a person who doesn't waste time. And I like a woman who doesn't hesitate to have a drink. Now, where is that goddam bartender?" She turned and waved at a man in a white shirt across the room. He scurried over.

"Scotch and water. No, make that neat." She turned to Dulcie. "So, do you have any news for me?"

Dulcie had prepared carefully. She actually did not have any news of the Micronesian bowl that Amelia wanted to buy. She had to tread lightly on that topic and move on quickly. "I've been speaking to a number of the trustees and I believe we're getting close to a decision to sell."

"Good! Good." Amelia stared out the window dreamily.

"There is still the stipulation that the bowl be loaned back to the museum for viewing purposes."

Amelia snapped back around. "What's that? Oh, yes. Of course. Couldn't that be worked out after the sale?"

Dulcie eyed her closely. '*She doesn't want to!* ' she suddenly thought. '*Once she has it, she doesn't want to give it up again. Even on loan!* ' She smiled at Amelia. "I'm afraid that the trustees would make it a condition of the sale. But there would only be a limited number of occasions when we would want it for display. And nearly all have been scheduled on our calendars already."

Amelia pursed her lips. She did not like this at all. "Yes, well, we can discuss this when the time comes." Secretly, she was considering offering more money in exchange for no loans. Once a piece was hers, she hated letting go.

"Of course," replied Dulcie. She sipped her wine to buy a little time so that she could change the subject. "I've heard that you're a collector of other works as well. Do you focus on any specific genre?" If Dulcie had learned nothing else about the elite class and the art world, she knew that they liked nothing better than to talk about themselves and their collections. She had found few exceptions to this rule.

The bartender approached with Amelia's drink. She swigged a very large mouthful. "Excellent," she said without looking at him. She turned back to Dulcie. "I collect what I like. No rhyme or reason other than that. I see something that strikes me, and I buy it."

Dulcie hoped that the general din around them masked her snort. She quickly took another sip of her own drink. "You're very fortunate to be able to have so many lovely pieces available to you. I'm surrounded by such beautiful art every day, but none of it is mine."

Amelia stared at her. What a thought! But then she remembered Dulcie's inheritance. "You've got money now, that's no secret. Why don't you buy something?"

Dulcie laughed. "My problem is that I wouldn't know where to begin. Plus, I would probably just hang it in my office and there it would be, still in the museum. Tell me, where do you display your works?"

For the second time Amelia stared at her. Display? Why would anyone but her need to see them? "Oh, I just tack them up here and there. Stick them on shelves."

Dulcie was beginning to understand Amelia's nature. She wasn't simply a collector. Amelia she was a hoarder. Dulcie wondered if Amelia even knew what she owned. "We've just gone through an exhaustive database update at the museum to make sure our inventory of works was correct. Do you keep a catalog of your pieces?" she asked innocently.

Amelia pointed to her head. "All up here. Well, I suppose the insurance company has one. Ross reports every piece that I buy to them, damn him. Still, I suppose if they went missing I'd appreciate some compensation."

Dulcie's immediate thought was, '*Would you know if anything went missing?*' She wasn't sure how to ask the question without insulting Amelia, so she let it go.

Amelia tossed back the rest of her scotch. "Good. Glad to hear there's progress on that bowl. Let me know when we're getting close. I'll get some funds transferred." She smiled hollowly at Dulcie, grabbed her purse and strode out of the bar.

The bartender appeared. "Can I get you another, Ma'am, or would you like the check now?" It was then Dulcie realized that Amelia fully expected Dulcie to pick up the bill. Well, Dulcie had extended the invitation after all, but the usual social niceties of "can I get this?" and "No, no! I invited you!" would have been appropriate. She sighed and reached for her purse.

Painting is easy when you don't know how,
but very difficult when you do.
~ Edgar Degas

CHAPTER FOURTEEN

Ross Davenport-Jones sat in his study and listened to the clocks tick. He had been doing quite a lot of that lately. Nothing was working for him except all of those steady, dependable clocks.

The police had questioned him that morning. Detective Nicholas Black had driven down from Portland to speak with him. Jennifer had been murdered, he had said. She'd been poisoned with ketamine. The detective knew that Ross was a veterinarian. And he knew full well that Ross had ketamine.

"Has anyone other than yourself had access to your medicine cabinet? ... Do you always keep it locked? ... Where are the keys kept? ... Do you ever carry ketamine with you in your medical bag? ... Do you leave your bag unguarded?" Ross knew exactly where the questions led. The world was closing in on him. The clocks were ticking away the hours, minutes, seconds, taunting him because they knew it was only a matter of time before everyone would know.

Something had to be done. He needed to either come clean or make his move. He knew he could not do the former. He would lose everything, including his practice. Being a vet was the only thing that made Ross truly happy. It was all that he had ever wanted. If that suddenly disappeared from his life, he would have no reason to wake up every morning.

He thought about Clark. Damn fool. Wasting his life. Ross had tried so many times to make something of him. Nothing seemed to take. And with the years passing, Ross realized that they had less and less in common. Sometimes he didn't even believe that Ross was actually his son.

Lydia. The image of her popped into his head without warning. Maybe she was the answer. Jennifer had failed him. He knew now that he had never truly trusted her. But Lydia seemed different. She always seemed so innocent and fresh. Could she be the solution?

Ross picked up his cell phone and looked up Clark's home number. The phone rang several times before anyone answered.

He heard Lydia's voice say, "Hello? Oh, Ross, it's you. Would you like to speak to Clark? He's not home right now."

Ross smiled for the first time in days. "No Lydia, it's actually you that I wanted to talk with."

Now, perhaps he was getting somewhere.

Ten minutes later, Lydia put down the phone as Clark walked in the door. She looked up at him. "That was your father," she said.

"Huh. Just missed him. That's too bad," he said without a hint of remorse.

"Actually, he wanted to talk to me."

"You?" Clark stopped and turned toward her. "Why?"

"Well, it seems he wants to buy me a horse."

&

Ross hopped out of the Land Rover. He felt buoyant. "This could actually work!" he said quietly to no one but himself. He took the front steps two at a time and rang the bell. In less than a minute he was comfortably seated in Donald Winter's overcrowded study.

"Jonsey!" Donald used his perpetual shout. "You sounded out of breath on the phone! What's up?"

Ross breathed deeply to calm himself. He counted to five before he spoke. "Sorry about that. I'd just finished loading up the car after a farm call. Things have been busy."

"Good for you!" Donald yelled. "Whattaya need?"

"I wanted to run something by you. The mare we talked about last time, Attagirl. You wanted to sell her. I've been looking for a gift for my new daughter-in-law, and this might be just the thing. She's talked about wanting to learn how to ride. I don't know what you're thinking of for a price, but...."

Donald Winters sat back in his chair and reached for the scotch, never more than arm's length away. "Gimme what ya got," he shouted, smiling.

Ross gave him a number on the low side of Attagirl's worth. He held his breath.

"Hmmm," said Donald. "I haven't heard back from that woman who was interested before, so I guess that's dead in the water." He poured a dram and swirled it, peering into the glass.

Ross felt a wave of panic begin to rise in his chest. Why had Donald used that phrase, 'dead in the water'? Did he know something?

Then Donald smiled at Ross over the rim of his glass and slapped his knee. "But, I'll be damned if we don't have a deal!" he hooted. He gestured to an empty glass beside him. "You have one too! We'll celebrate!" He poured the scotch and handed it to Ross.

Ross tried to stay calm. He was grateful for the drink. It was an effective distraction. "Thank you," he simply said, not indicating if he meant the drink or the horse.

"I'll call up my lawyer. Draw up the papers. You do what you need to do. I'll take a check or whatever you like. I know you're as honest as they come, Jonsey!" He plunked his empty glass down loudly on the metal tray beside him making the scotch bottle tip precariously.

Ross knew it was his cue to leave. He tossed back his drink in one gulp, shook Donald Winter's hand and nearly ran out of the room.

Lexi had finished her ride several minutes earlier and had quietly entered the house, knowing that her uncle was talking with Ross Davenport-Jones. She had seen his Land Rover outside. Of course she had heard every word. She watched from the shadow of the staircase as the front door closed behind him. Her mind worked quickly. This was interesting information. How to use it was the question.

She silently slipped from the house when Ross had driven away and slid behind the wheel of her car. Carefully, thoughtfully, she made her way along the winding roads and back into the city of Boston.

∞

"What did you tell her?" Lexi asked, sipping her coffee in bed, her blond hair perfectly tousled.

"Tell who?" Clark said lazily from beside her as he blew on the top of his own coffee.

"Your wife?"

His hand jerked and he spilled coffee on the sheet. "Dammit! Sorry."

"Never mind that," Lexi said. "What did you say?"

"I just said I had to talk with my parents and might as well stay down with them."

Lexi's smile was incredulous. "And she bought that?"

"She seemed to. She said it was fine, that she was thinking of seeing her mother."

"And you bought that?"

"Lexi, what do you care? I'm here. That's what you wanted. Right?"

Lexi did not know what she wanted any more. For the first time, she actually began to think that the way she was leading her life might not be quite right. She pushed the idea from her mind.

"Of course, darling! That's exactly what I wanted!" She held her cup toward him. "Now be a dear and get me some more coffee?"

Without hesitating, Ross took both of their cups and left the room. Lexi shook her head. This was just too easy.

❤

Nicholas Black drove north toward Portland. He liked long drives. He never played the radio or listened to anything. He preferred the silence. They sky was deep blue and crystal clear. His thoughts were not.

Nick's mind wandered through his conversations with all of the suspects. He had finished interviews with everyone for the time being. Now they all knew that Jennifer was murdered. "This is when things could start to get interesting," he said out loud.

Considering everyone, Ross Davenport-Jones had seemed the most nervous. Nick knew that he was definitely hiding something. Not unusual, certainly. Everyone had something to hide. Ross's reactions had been something more, though. Nick needed to find out more about him.

Amelia had been the opposite. Cool. Controlled. She had looked slightly surprised to hear that Jennifer had been murdered, but quickly went back to her perpetual self-centered manner. When he had mentioned the ketamine, she had said, "You know my husband's a vet. He uses the stuff, I'm sure. Not that he'd ever have the guts to do something like kill someone."

Lydia was still on Nick's list. He thought it unlikely that she had killed her sister, but he had seen it happen before. Fits of jealousy. Moments of rage. Old family rivalries. It would not be the first time.

Then there was Clark Davenport-Jones. He had been interesting. "Smooth" was the first word that came to Nick's mind. Clark had certainly had time to prepare. Nick was not able to interview him until well after everyone else.

What puzzled Nick most, however, was the art. Everything about the case seemed so personal. Jennifer's death had been carefully planned. If the murderer took that much trouble, and risk, to bring about her death, why did Jennifer still have the van Gogh? Certainly someone who planned so carefully would have made sure that they were able to get the painting. What did the art have to do with it all? Did it have anything to do with it? Maybe it was completely unrelated to Jennifer's death? Nick couldn't convince himself that they were two isolated yet coincidental incidents.

He pulled into the station and saw his partner's car. '*Coffee with Johnson. That's what's in order,*' he thought. He found Adam Johnson at his desk in the perpetual position: leaning back, feet up, eyes closed. "Hey!" Nick said loudly. "Not gettin' anything done like that!"

Johnson opened his eyes slowly. "I happen to be contemplating a case. They require thought and consideration. Maybe you should try it instead of having your ass in the car running around all the time."

Nick just laughed. "Why don't you get your ass out of that chair and let's go get a coffee."

Johnson was up in a flash. "You buyin'?"

Nick grinned. "Always, it seems."

They walked to Roasters, got coffee in addition to a cheese danish for Johnson, and were about to slide into their usual booth when Dulcie came through the door. "There's your girlfriend," Johnson grunted as he eased himself onto the seat.

"Okay, she's not my…."

Dulcie had spotted them and was already within earshot.

"Hi guys. Mind if I join you? I've just found out something interesting."

"No problem," said Johnson. "Nick, slide over and make some room for the lady."

"Let me go get a coffee first," said Dulcie and continued over to the counter.

Nick glared at his partner. "Do *not* start! We're on a case. Don't distract me!" Johnson just chuckled and stuffed a large piece of danish into his mouth.

Dulcie came back and slid in next to Nick. "This may or may not be interesting but it seems like a pretty big coincidence."

"What's that?" asked Nick.

"I keep reaching dead-ends with the ownership of the two works that we found under the lobster trap. I did find out, however, that Amelia Davenport-Jones likes to collect a variety of things. And a gallery owner I spoke with in Boston all but admitted that she bought a Cocteau poster."

Nick was thoughtful. "Are you sure it was the same one? You said that there were multiple copies."

"Yes, but everything else seems to be accounted for, in this region anyway. I checked on the provenance for each. No minor task. Fortunately, I have a small army of interns to do my bidding. Plus, it'd be a pretty big coincidence if two identical works were sold in the same city at the same time."

"True." Nick looked over at his partner.

Johnson polished off the last of the danish, washing it down with swig of coffee. "I'm with her," he said, raising his cup to Dulcie. "Too big a coincidence. Question is then, how'd it get into the hands of little Miss Jennifer so she could stick it in a tube and hide it underwater?"

The lightening bolt hit Nick and Dulcie at the same moment. "Lydia took it!" they said simultaneously.

Johnson grinned. "My thoughts exactly," he said calmly as he delicately wiped the crumbs from his mouth with a paper napkin.

ᙅ

The purchase of Attagirl had gone through quickly. Before he knew it, Ross was the new owner, along with Lydia of course. He had made sure his name was on the paperwork. Lydia looked at the mare standing out in the paddock and wondered if this was such a good idea.

She had never ridden a horse before. "The rich ride," her sister had told her. Jennifer had wanted her to learn. "Just get the basics so you can talk about it somewhat intelligently at one of those damned cocktail parties."

Clark sat astride another horse, holding the reigns of Attagirl. "Just slide your foot into the stirrup, grab the front of the saddle, and in one quick motion swing your leg up and over," Lydia heard Ross say.

She let him guide her foot into the stirrup. Ross said, "Okay, on the count of three. One, two, three…"

He lifted Lydia by the waist and she swung her leg around.

'*That wasn't so bad,*' she thought.

As she settled her weight back into the saddle, however, Attagirl made a strange noise. Then, neighing loudly, she bucked, her front legs flailing in front of her. The reigns instantly slipped from Clark's hands.

Lydia felt herself flying backward through the air, then felt her helmet slam against something very hard. She saw the stables spinning around her, and the world went black.

The light slowly filtered back into her mind as Lydia opened her eyes. She was in a hospital room. No one was around. Her head was throbbing. She tried to speak but nothing came out. Frantically she clawed at the tubes and wires and buttons around her looking for something that would call a nurse.

The doctor walked in the room seconds before Lydia was about to pull out her IV. "Whoa there!" she said. "You're awake! You're safe and you'll be fine! Let's just lie back down here," she spoke calmly and, seeing Lydia struggling with it, pulled the blanket up over her. "Do you know your name?"

Lydia's body crumpled back onto the pillows. "Lydia Hully. I mean, Lydia Davenport-Jones." She began to cry.

"Shhh. You're okay, but you do have a concussion. They tell me you were airborne for a few seconds! Do you want me to call someone for you? I think your husband and your father-in-law just went for a coffee."

"No!" said Lydia, almost fearfully. "Don't tell them I'm awake!" She thought for several moments. "I know. Is my cell phone around? I know who I can call."

The doctor looked slightly confused, but reached into a drawer and located Lydia's phone. Lydia took it quickly, looked up a number, and dialed.

"It's Lydia. I'm in the hospital. I need to talk to you. Can you come over here now?" Then she simply thanked the person on the other end of the line and clicked off the phone. "My head really hurts," she whispered, dropping the phone on the bed in front of her.

"I can imagine," said the doctor as she checked Lydia's pulse. Do you want more medicine for it? We can increase your dose a little in the drip." She gestured toward the IV.

"Will it make me drowsy?" asked Lydia.

"Yes, it will," the doctor replied.

"Then I don't want it yet. I have to talk to somebody. When I'm done, then yes, I'd like some more."

"No problem," the doctor smiled. "Why don't you press this," she slid a plastic call button into Lydia's hand, "when you're ready. Should I put your phone back in the drawer?"

Lydia nodded, then winced. Moving her head at all hurt.

"Yes, try not to move your head any more than necessary," said the doctor as she left.

'*Now you tell me,*' thought Lydia.

Dulcie walked quickly down the hallway, checking room numbers. She had already called Nick. He was on his way. At last she found Lydia.

As she came through the door, Lydia looked up. For a split second her face was contorted in fear, then it relaxed as she saw Dulcie.

"Thank God, it's you!" she said. "Don't let them in here!"

Dulcie looked confused. "Don't let who in?"

Lydia was shaking. "Clark. And Ross," she said simply. "They tried to kill me."

"What?" The word had burst out of Dulcie's mouth before she could stop it.

"I know. It's crazy. But I think they tried to kill me. Ross, my father-in-law, gave me a horse. I don't know why. I'd mentioned riding but wasn't really that serious. He gave me the horse and then they convinced me to go for a ride with Clark. He was already on his horse. Ross helped me up, but as soon as I sat down in the saddle, the horse bucked. She'd seemed so gentle. It was like someone had kicked her or something. I went flying off, hit my head, and I woke up here."

Dulcie did not know what to think. "But if they wanted you dead, why did they bring you here?"

Tears began to stream down Lydia's face. "That isn't all. I have to tell you something. I can't keep it a secret any longer. I think Jen might have already told you anyway, since your phone number was on her hand. I took the artwork. From my mother-in-law. I took them, Jen hid them, then we sold them. At first I did it out of spite. Then I did it because I knew Amelia hated me and Clark was cheating on me!" Lydia lowered her voice to a whisper. "I think it was with that awful woman who just appeared at Jennifer's funeral. Alexia Kent." She put her hands to her face and sobbed. "It's so humiliating! What have I done? What's going to happen now? Help me, please!"

Dulcie handed her a box of tissues. A slight noise from the hallway made Dulcie turn. She saw Nick standing there, just out of Lydia's sight. He put his finger to his lips.

"Wow. That's a lot to confess, Lydia. But it doesn't explain why they would want to kill you. Does it?"

Lydia snuffled her nose into a fresh wad of tissues and looked out the window. "No, not really. Nothing makes sense any more."

She looked very small in the hospital bed. Very small, and very weak. Dulcie thought, '*She needs rest, and not just from that bump on her head.*'

"Let me get a doctor or nurse, and see what they can do for you. Would you like me to have someone stay with you?" she asked.

"Yes. I'm afraid," she said simply. She held up the call button in her hand. "The doctor said to push this when I wanted her to come back," she added, "and I can get more medicine for the pain. My head hurts so badly."

"All right then. Go ahead and push it. I'll wait here until the doctor comes. And Lydia," Dulcie reached out and took her hand. "You've been through a lot. More than just hitting your head, or your sister's death. You need to rest and maybe talk with someone when you're ready."

Lydia held Dulcie's hand tightly until the doctor arrived.

In the hallway, Dulcie rubbed her hand. Lydia's grip felt like it had stopped the circulation. "Did you hear all of that?" she asked Nick.

"Uh huh. I think so. Let's get out of here."

"Do you think she's in danger?" asked Dulcie.

"I've got a guard here already." He pointed to a man standing quietly behind Dulcie. "Thanks, Jack. I'll send someone to replace you in a couple hours."

"No problem," the man replied.

Dulcie and Nick quickly left the building by the side stairs. Dulcie began to speak but he stopped her. "Not here," he said. They made their way out, and silently walked down the street. "Want to go to my house?" asked Dulcie. "We're closest to it right now."

Nick nodded. As soon as they were inside her house, Nick was on his phone. First he called the guard at the hospital to see if Clark and Ross had returned. They had not. Then he called Adam Johnson. Nothing new to report from him.

"Got any coffee?" Nick asked. "I need to clear my head."

Dulcie quickly made coffee and they sat at the table. "That was quite a confession from Lydia, and it explains the paintings," she said.

"Two of them anyway. The van Gogh is still a mystery. Lydia couldn't have possibly taken that."

Dulcie sipped her coffee. She had made it strong and it seemed to filter into her mind almost instantly. "Why would Lydia suddenly jump to the conclusion that Ross and Clark were trying to kill her? Why not just assume it was an accident?" she mused.

"Do you think it was?" asked Nick.

"I'm not totally convinced," said Dulcie. "But I just don't see why they wouldn't want her around. Did she know something?"

Nick drained his mug. "Is there more?" he asked. Dulcie reached for his mug, but he stood up. "No, no. I'll get it."

Dulcie heard him rummaging around in the kitchen. He came back in and sat down, cradling the cup in both hands. "Okay!" He looked intently into the steaming liquid. "Okay," he said again more softly. "We have Jennifer dead with your phone number on her hand, two artworks that belonged to Amelia but were stolen by Lydia, and a van Gogh that was stolen by a person or persons unknown from a random couple in Boston."

"Right," said Dulcie. "Should I be writing this down?"

Nick's laugh was humorless. "Not yet. Let's just walk through. Next we have Lydia thrown from a horse that Ross bought for her. Both he and Clark were getting her up on it when the accident happened. Jennifer was poisoned with ketamine that Ross had on hand. Clark, or his mother for that matter, could easily have taken it, though. So the primary suspects all appear to be from the Davenport-Jones family."

"Although, there's one outside chance of another," said Dulcie.

"Not you!" exclaimed Nick. "I know your number was on her hand, but I'm pretty sure that…."

Dulcie put up her hand to silence him, smiling. "Thank you for the vote of confidence. No, I was referring to someone else who may have had a motive to kill Lydia at least. Did you hear Lydia in the hospital telling me that Clark hadn't been faithful to her?"

"Yes, but she was speaking too softly for me to hear the rest."

"Well, she told me the name. It's the woman that you spoke with after the funeral. You said your families had been friends. Alexia Kent, I think her name is?"

Nick flinched so hard that his coffee spilled. Dulcie jumped up and grabbed a towel from the kitchen. She threw it at him as she said, "Wow, struck a nerve there! Did you have a revelation? Is she the murderer?"

Nick focused on cleaning the coffee from the table. "I don't know," he said quietly. "It does add another angle." He looked intently at Dulcie. "Does Lydia know for sure?"

Dulcie nodded. "I think so. I don't know if she has absolute proof, but she seemed very sure."

Nick stood and went into the kitchen. He rinsed his coffee mug in the sink. "I should get going. I have to check back in with Johnson before he heads home for the day. You need anything?"

Dulcie shook her head. "No, I think I'm fine. I don't think my life is in danger, certainly. I'll let you know if I think of anything else," she said.

"Good. I'll call you later. Lock this," He jerked his head toward the door, then quietly closed it behind him.

I'll call you. How many times had Dulcie heard that line before? But in the case of Nick, it was always true. He always did.

For me, painting is a way to forget life.
It is a cry in the night,
a strangled laugh.
~ Georges Rouault

CHAPTER FIFTEEN

At some point during the night, Dulcie had awakened and began turning the events over again in her mind. The thought occurred to her that she should be looking at everything differently. They had been focused on Jennifer, Lydia, and the two artworks that she and Nick had found. The van Gogh seemed like an outlier. "What if," Dulcie said out loud, "What if that's the key?"

Sitting in her office at the museum several hours later, Dulcie opened her computer and brought up an image of the painting. "Beautiful," she murmured. "I can't imagine owning something like this." She realized that now she did in fact have the money to own something like that, but only just. "It would be gone in a flash, all on one painting!" she said out loud.

She checked the provenance. It all seemed perfectly plausible. On a whim, she called the auction house that had sold the work. She knew several people there and perhaps could get some additional thoughts.

"Claire! It's Dulcie, how are you? …Great! I have a question for you. I'm looking up some van Gogh information and wondered if I could find out anything more about that piece that was stolen from the couple in Boston, you know the one? …Yes, that's it. Sure, call me back. Thanks!"

Dulcie hunched over her computer for the next hour typing in every web search that she could think of, clicking link after link about the theft. The couple was perplexed as to how it was stolen. The wife was very upset since it had been a gift that she had dearly wanted. The police could find nothing for leads. Cleaning staff, security people, even closed circuit television had all lead to dead ends.

The phone rang again. "Hi Claire," Dulcie answered. "OK… yes, that's interesting. …hmmm… Wait a minute. What did you say? Who? Are you sure? …Yes, thanks!" she nearly forgot to end the call before dialing Nick's number.

Ten minutes later he walked into her office.

"Close the door," she said without looking up. She was staring at an image of the van Gogh painting on her computer. She looked up at him with the same intense gaze. "When is a theft not a theft?" she asked.

He looked at her quizzically. "Is this a trick question?"

"Sort of. Do you have an answer?"

"Um, when it's a joke? Or a misunderstanding? Or just something lost?"

"Or fraud," she said quietly. She let the words sink in.

Nick's brain began whirring slowly, then faster and faster. "They did it!" He said at last. "They stole it themselves! They collected on the insurance!"

"Absolutely. Very clever, but not very original. Insurance companies take great pains to investigate. But this couple must have done an excellent job. They got away with it."

"Or nearly did. But what do we have for proof?"

"How about this?" Dulcie told him about her conversation with the auction house. Nick was silent. He let the words flow over him. He closed his eyes. Yes, it was the simplest solution. It all came together. He opened his eyes and stood up.

"I need to get a search warrant. I'll talk later." He quickly strode form the room, then poked his head back in. "Dulcie, thanks! You're an angel!"

Dulcie waited for him to leave, then sat back in her chair and spun around. "Yep, all in a day's work, my friends! All in a day's work!" She said to the empty room, grinning all the while.

∝

Clark returned home with his father, to find the police thoroughly rummaging through his belongings. "What's going on here?" he shouted. Ross stood beside him, unable to speak.

"We have a warrant, sir," the officer handed him a piece of paper. Nick grabbed it, crumpled it up, and threw it over his shoulder behind him.

"I don't care what you have! What the hell are you looking for? My wife's in the hospital for Chrissake!"

"I'll call your mother," said Ross, finally regaining his voice. It was all he could think of to do. He went back outside.

Clark fumed watching the police go through his personal things as though they were browsing in a store, picking up each item, turning it over, putting it back. He saw two of them taking pictures. "This is an invasion of my privacy!" he yelled to no one in particular.

From the bedroom he heard a woman's voice shout, "Got it!"

Nicholas Black came out of the bathroom where he had been analyzing the medicine cabinet. Clark glared at him. Nick continued into the bedroom. "Perfect. Show me where it was," Clark heard him say.

Nick came back out. "Clark Davenport-Jones, I'm placing you under arrest for the murder of Jennifer Hully and the attempted murder of Lydia Davenport-Jones." He glanced at one of the other policemen. "Read him his rights."

"What! Are you kidding me? I didn't kill anyone!" The officer was droning on as Clark continued to shout. A second policeman quickly put his wrists in handcuffs. Running out of breath, Clark was silent for a moment, the gravity of the situation descending upon him.

"Oh, and I'll need this." Nick began to reach into Clark's pants pocket but thought better of it. "Jill, a hand here?"

The officer who had yelled from the other room stifled a laugh, stuffed her hand deep into Clark's pocket, and pulled out his cell phone. "I'm assuming this is what you were after?" She smirked. It was well known that Nick had not been seen with a woman since he began work with the Portland Police Force. A few rumors had begun to spread that his preference was in the other direction. Nick ignored her comment and took the phone.

Ross Davenport-Jones came back in. "Did I hear you yelling? *Clark*!? What the hell is...?" He trailed off upon seeing his son in handcuffs. A look of complete despair washed over his face. "Clark? What have you done?"

Clark was now even more furious that his own father would assume that he had done anything at all. If he had not killed anyone before, he was ready to now.

"Take him in," said Nick quietly. Two policemen walked him out the door and slid him into the back of a cruiser.

Nick heard Clark say, "For God sake, don't turn on the damn blue lights! If the neighbors see anything..." The car door slammed and the cruiser swiftly backed out, blue lights flashing.

Ross hadn't moved. "What's going on?" he finally managed to croak.

"I'm sorry to tell you, Mr. Davenport-Jones, but we found this among your son's things." He held up a vial of liquid. "Do you know what it is?"

Ross did not even have to look. He had seen it hundreds of times in his bag. "Yes," he said hoarsely, "that's ketamine."

The lights in Lydia's hospital room were low, a soft warm glow that mirrored the evening sun outside.

Dulcie listened to her steady breathing. She had hoped to speak to Lydia again, but did not want to wake her.

As she was about to leave, she heard Lydia shift slightly on the bed. She looked over. Lydia's eyes fluttered open. She turned her head to look at Dulcie, and winced.

"Sorry," said Dulcie. "Try not to move your head."

"Easier said than done," Lydia replied. "Why are you here? Oh, I'm sorry. That sounded rude, didn't it."

Dulcie smiled and shook her head. "First of all, I wanted to check on you. You seemed pretty scared the last time I saw you. Are you still scared?"

"Not as much," Lydia replied softly. "They have a guard outside, don't they?"

"Yes. I confess that when you called me down here the first time, I immediately called Detective Black. He didn't want to take any chances."

Lydia reached for a glass of water. Dulcie quickly handed it to her.

"Has anything happened?" she said between sips. A strange sense of doom had come over her.

"Yes. Are you sure you want to know?"

"I have to know," Lydia said.

"Your husband has been arrested for your sister's murder and for your attempted murder." Whatever reaction Dulcie had expected from Lydia, she was not prepared for what she heard next.

"Good. But the little bastard didn't do it."

Dulcie leaned forward. "I know," she said simply.

A large tear rolled down Lydia's cheek.

"Lydia, tell me one more thing. Was your sister dyslexic?"

Lydia looked confused, but nodded slightly. She put her hand to her head as the pain shot through again.

"That's all. Please go easy on yourself. You were caught in a spiral. Truly. Now try to get some sleep again."

Lydia attempted a smile but failed. She simply closed her eyes.

ന്ദ

Amelia Davenport-Jones screeched up the highway toward Portland. "*They're all a bunch of idiots,*" she thought. "*Especially that worthless spawn. No interests other than screwing anyone but his wife. Although that's not necessarily bad. The longer they go without children, the easier it will be for me to convince him to divorce her. Little gold-digging bitch.*" She nearly spat on the steering wheel.

Clark's father. What had she ever seen in him? Well, his money for one thing. That certainly did not hurt. But she couldn't deny that knowing he was a pushover had also been immensely appealing. She had known from the beginning that she could convince him of anything and do whatever she wanted, without interference.

It had been nice at first. But she had not counted on what the lack of respect would do to their relationship. Increasingly she saw him as a sniveling, whining, annoying coward. Every time she pushed him and he caved, her disgust grew. He was no better than a dog. No, actually, a dog was better. At least they didn't talk back, which Ross had somehow found the courage to do on occasion.

Amelia took the highway exit for Scarborough and made her way out to Prouts Neck. The lights were on in some of the houses. She could see people inside, talking, laughing. She imagined Clark's arrest was the topic of conversation on everyone's lips.

Amelia saw Ross's car in the driveway. She pulled in beside it. The house was dark. Strange. She got out and closed the car door gently, then went up the steps to the back door. She opened it slowly. "Ross?" she said quietly. Part of her had the gleaming hope that he had committed suicide and she would find his body on the floor.

As she shut the door behind her, the lights blazed on. Amelia blinked, stunned, then glared around the room at the people seated in front of her. Her ridiculous husband, that damned detective, the annoying museum woman... then she realized that Clark was sitting there as well. "What the hell is going on?"

"Come sit down with us, honey," said Ross. She couldn't remember the last time he had addressed her with any kind of endearment. He stood and took her hand, which she quickly yanked away. "All right then," he said. "You can stand there and tell us how you did it."

Amelia blinked. She opened her mouth. Nothing came out. She closed it. Then, without warning, she burst out laughing. She laughed and laughed and could not stop. Her sides ached. She collapsed into the chair next to her and continued to giggle uncontrollably.

At last, finally able to speak again, she said. "You are all such imbeciles!" This brought on more gales of laughter.

Nick was not amused. "We certainly are," he said. "Such imbeciles that you got away with it, right?"

Amelia straightened up, still smiling. "Well, I nearly got away with it!" She tried to suppress another giggle.

"Why don't you tell us how it happened, from the beginning?" Nick said.

Amelia turned to him. "If you're so damned smart, why don't you tell me!"

Nick looked at her coldly. "All right. Let's start with the van Gogh."

"Oohh! Great place to start!" Amelia chimed in.

"You had wanted it from the beginning, didn't you? But the bidding went too high, even for you. You lost out. But, just after the purchase the couple who did buy it learned that they had just suffered a huge financial loss. They planned the theft and collected on the insurance.

"That's where Jennifer came in. Somehow they knew her, although we haven't determined exactly who introduced them. Jennifer loved risks. She agreed to hide the painting for a time, then she would return it to them when everything had blown over. They paid her well. She devised the idea of putting it underwater. Brilliant, to be sure."

Amelia smirked. "Brilliant except for the fact that I overheard her talking to her sister about it. Not directly, of course, but I put it all together."

"So that's when you decided that you had to have it, right? It didn't matter to you that no one else would know, or be able to see it. The painting would be all yours. The premier work of your entire collection."

Amelia looked dreamy. "And it wasn't going to cost me a cent!"

Nick looked disgusted. "This is where I lose your twisted logic, however. If it wasn't going to cost you a cent, how would you convince Jennifer to hand it over to you?"

Amelia turned to her son. "That's where you come in, you worthless idiot."

"What?" Clark heard his voice nearly screech. "I had nothing to do with it!"

"Yes you did, but you just didn't know it. That night when you and Jennifer were having drinks? I saw you. I was there. And I saw you leave with her. I followed you, and watched you get on the boat. It didn't take a genius to figure out why the two of you were out there. That's why I planted the ketamine in your desk drawer, dear son. To teach you a lesson. I just thought Lydia would find it first and think you killed her sister. Stupid girl respects your privacy too much, evidently."

"So you used emotional blackmail on Jennifer. You threatened to tell Lydia that her dear sister had an affair with her husband," Nick said.

"I wasn't her husband yet," Clark muttered.

"Tell that to Lydia," Dulcie chimed in. She wanted to slap him.

Nick stood and paced the room. "You must have gone diving with Jennifer, and that's how you got the ketamine on her mouthpiece."

Ross snapped his head around to stare at his wife. "Wait a minute! You don't dive! You hate swimming!"

Amelia began laughing again. A shrieking, piercing laugh. "For a van Gogh? I'd do anything! Jennifer agreed to go fetch the painting in that tube underwater. She had to, of course, but she wouldn't go alone. Do you know how easy it is to learn how to dive? I did it in a week. That's when I knew what I would do. It would look like an accident."

"But how did you get the ketamine on her equipment?" asked Nick.

"It was so easy! I distracted her, of course. I dropped my mask by the car. I made her go back and get it. Then I told her to check my equipment to make sure I'd done everything right. It was easy to drip the ketamine on anything her mouth would come into contact with, then just mold some of that wax over it to keep it there long enough. It worked so well!"

"But then everything started to fall apart, right?" asked Nick.

Amelia sneered. "She put one over on me. Or tried. I was going to follow her, let her get the painting, and when the drug started working, just take it and swim away. I stuck to her like glue while we swam out, but when she picked up that lobster trap and pulled out the tube she started kicking up sand and silt from the bottom. I couldn't see her very well. The sun was going down too, so it was getting darker. I lost her. I was so mad. I swam around until I couldn't see any more. Then I went in."

Ross looked horrified. "And left her out there to die in that cold, black water?"

Amelia said nothing. She looked out the window at the ocean. It was a very dark night, no moon, just billions of stars piercing the sky. It reminded her of the other van Gogh, *Starry Night*, infinitely more famous than the one she had nearly managed to snare. *Starry Night*. She would love to have that one, too, if only....

Suddenly, she knew that it would never be enough. She would never be able to stop her habit, never be satisfied with what she had. There would always be something else. Something unattainable. Something beyond impossible. And she had already killed for something far less worthy.

Amelia bolted out the back door before anyone realized what she was doing. Nick thought she was heading for one of the cars, trying to escape. Then he realized that she was running toward the beach.

Dulcie felt she could read Amelia's mind. She knew instantly where Amelia was going. She raced after her but the woman had a large head start and was surprisingly agile for her age. She plunged into the water. Dulcie dove in after her.

"No!" shouted Nick. He lunged after Dulcie. A wave caught them both and threw them off their feet. Dulcie felt it crash over her, dark, cold, clawing at her.

A hand gripped her arm and yanked her up. An arm wrapped tightly around her. She heard Nick's voice in her ear, "We've lost her already. It's too dark. I won't lose you, too! I won't lose you!" His voice trailed off in a whisper.

Dulcie coughed and gagged from the seawater she had nearly inhaled. Nick had her pressed against him, both arms around her, half dragging, half carrying her back onto the beach. At last he let her stand, but he did not let go.

"Get her a blanket!" she heard him yell. Dulcie dropped to her knees and wretched on the sand, grateful that it was very dark and the waves were loud. She saw Clark running toward them with a blanket. Ross simply stood on the beach, staring out at the sea.

"Is she gone?" he said at last. His lips barely moved. "Is she really gone?"

Nick had wrapped the blanket around Dulcie and helped her to her feet. They stumbled toward the house. Clark put his arm around his father's shoulders and guided him back. Nick heard him say, "Yes, Dad. I think she is. She's finally gone."

❧

As he drove back to his apartment, still dripping from the unexpected dash into the ocean, Nick listened to the message that he had recorded from Clark's cell phone one more time. Finally, this was it. This was what he had been waiting for, hoping to find, for nearly six years. It would put an end to everything holding him back. He had his proof. He could finally move on.

☙

Lydia had made steady and rapid progress. Dulcie sat next to her in the hospital room, telling her about everything that had happened. When she finished, Lydia said, "There's just one thing that I don't understand. Why did Jennifer have your phone number written on her hand? She never called you, did she?"

"No," said Dulcie. "She didn't. That was one of the most confusing parts of this whole ordeal. Finally I realized why. Remember when I asked you if she was dyslexic? It confirmed what I had guessed. The number she had meant to write was Amelia's. Our phone numbers are very similar, they just have a couple of digits switched. She probably had written it down in case she needed to call Amelia at the last minute about the dive. I didn't put it all together until someone at the museum asked me for my phone number. You never really think about your own. I just rattled it off, then I began to think that it sounded like another number I'd called recently. I was right." Dulcie explained.

"Why did Amelia plant the ketamine in Clark's desk, though? He's her only child. How could a mother do something like that?" Lydia asked.

Dulcie sighed. "I think that Amelia was angry about a number of things. One of them was the mess her son had made of his life."

"Like marrying me," Lydia said quietly.

"Yes, that was one thing that annoyed Amelia, for sure, but there's more. Lydia, what I'm about to tell you may not be easy to hear. Is that all right?"

Lydia looked at her with concern but nodded.

Dulcie continued. "Before you and Clark were married, he had a fling with Jennifer. Or I should say, he nearly had a fling with Jennifer. Evidently he was too drunk to do anything."

Lydia looked upset. "That can't be true! Jennifer would never... would never hurt me like that!" She gulped loudly.

Dulcie gently put her hand on Lydia's arm. "We don't know Jennifer's reasoning. Maybe she was just testing him to see if he was worthy of you. Maybe she wanted to have something to hold over him if he ever tried to hurt you, or divorce you and leave you with nothing. Or maybe Jennifer was just being Jennifer and taking one of her risks. We simply don't know. What we do know is that Amelia saw them and used that as blackmail to get Jennifer to go on that last dive. I also think that Clark's indiscretion added to Amelia's growing dislike for him."

Lydia looked out the window. "Yes, Jennifer must have had a good reason," she whispered. "Jennifer would never hurt me."

Dulcie gave her a moment to process everything. "I'm sure you're right. She wouldn't. But it did give Amelia another reason to despise her son. In the end she had only two choices. She could pin the blame on Clark, or on her husband. I'm sure she would have preferred blaming Ross but she didn't have enough evidence against him. Besides, sending her son to prison would get you out of the picture too."

"What puzzles me," Dulcie continued, "is how Jennifer got the tubes with the artworks under the lobster trap in the first place. You said that she never went diving alone. How could she have done that with no one seeing her?"

Lydia laughed softly. "I had the same question. And of course, Jennifer always had an answer. She had worked off and on for a marine salvage company. When she went diving with a buddy and had to access a tube, she told them that the company was doing some testing of containers. She even offered the other divers something for 'helping her with her work' like filling up their air tank, just to make it seem legitimate. She thought of everything. Well, almost everything." Lydia shivered and pulled the covers around her more tightly. "Do you really think that what happened to me was actually an accident?" she asked.

"I'm sure of it."

"Then why did the detective put a guard at my door?"

"Just to be certain. At that point, he didn't want to take chances. It also helped you to rest more easily so that you could heal."

"That is true, it did help." She fingered the edge of the sheet lying over her. "I don't ever want to see any of them again. I'm going to get a divorce, you know."

Dulcie nearly laughed. "I think that was pretty obvious! But what are you going to do after that?"

Lydia looked away. "I was going to ask you the same question," she said quietly.

Dulcie was confused. "What do you mean?"

"I mean that you will probably have to turn me in. I stole from my mother-in-law. I stole from the family, basically. And I sold her artwork illegally."

"Does anyone else besides me know?" asked Dulcie.

Lydia shook her head. "I didn't tell anyone. I don't think Jennifer did either. She wouldn't, to protect me. I didn't even know exactly where she hid the artworks. She told me that they were underwater and safe. I thought she was crazy to do that, but it worked."

"Lydia, the way I see it, you are part of the Davenport-Jones family, for a bit longer anyway. And your mother-in-law is most likely dead. You may not have obtained the artwork and carried out the sales in the most straightforward manner, but there doesn't really seem to be a crime committed. Not as far as I'm concerned. I don't see any reason why it shouldn't just remain in the past, easily forgotten. I mean, you never misrepresented who the artists were, so no fraud was committed. The way I see it, you simply withheld provenance information. That could be corrected. I really don't see Clark or Ross pressing charges against you at this point for theft, do you?"

Lydia smiled. "No. No, I don't." She looked shyly at Dulcie. "It was wrong, I know. I shouldn't have done it. I was so hurt and confused and depressed and…."

"I know. We all can do strange things when we're put in strange situations. I think you've suffered through enough, however." Dulcie looked at her watch. "And now I have to go. I have to make one last stop this evening before it gets too late."

"Thanks for seeing me, Dulcie. Can we talk again sometime?"

"Of course," Dulcie smiled. "Any time."

ᘒ

Dulcie knocked on the door of Nick's apartment, a bottle of the pinot noir that she knew he liked cradled in her arm. She was looking forward to recapping the entire case with him and had decided to drop by. She wore jeans, espadrilles, an old cotton sweater. She was comfortable with Nick. She had been thinking about talking with him, hearing his voice, all day.

She knocked on the door again. From the other side, she heard an odd clicking. What was that sound? She knew it. As the door opened she realized what it was. High heels. She stared at a pair of expensive stiletto pumps, then her eyes travelled up two long legs encased in a buttery leather pencil skirt, followed by a silk blouse, then blonde hair waving artfully. Alexia Kent smiled at her condescendingly.

"Oh!" was all that Dulcie could say.

"You didn't expect me here, did you?" Lexi said, tossing her hair over her shoulder.

"Well, no. But I know your family and Nick's were friends, and you knew the Davenport-Joneses, so I guess…" Dulcie knew she was babbling.

A haughty, superior laugh erupted from Lexi. "Friends? Is that what he told you? I suppose you could say that."

"Lexi, did I hear someone at the door?" Nick appeared behind her. When he saw Dulcie, his face fell. His mouth opened to speak but nothing came out.

"Yes," continued Lexi. "I suppose you could say we're *friends* of sorts. You see, darling Dulcie," she paused, "I'm his wife."

A wave of nausea flooded over Dulcie. She shoved the bottle of wine at Lexi and managed to blurt, "Enjoy." Then she turned and walked away as quickly as possible, forcing herself not to run. Lexi's arrogant laughter rang out behind her, taunting her.

Dulcie thought she heard Nick call out her name, but she didn't look back. She was not going to look back.

THE
FRAGILE
FLOWER

KERRY J CHARLES

The Dulcie Chambers
Museum Mysteries
Book #3

THE FRAGILE FLOWER

CHAPTER ONE

"They call it *Young Man's Death*."

The voice slid softly down the back of Dulcie's neck. It wasn't a whisper or a murmur, but the gentle melodious voice of a woman who had lived in Bermuda for a lifetime. Dulcie turned slowly and smiled. "Do you know why?"

The woman laughed, a beautiful, low sound like the turquoise waves rushing against the shore nearby. "It is a name from the old country. My grandmother was English. I visited her in Cornwall when I was a very little girl. Once, I picked this flower," she gestured toward the painting on the wall behind Dulcie. "My grandmother, she gasped and said, 'Cassandra, do you have a boyfriend? Because if you do, he is in big trouble now!' Of course then I made her explain it all. They say that if a girl picks this flower, her lover will die."

"Did you believe it?" Dulcie asked.

The woman shook her head gently. "Of course not! First, I did not have a boyfriend. Second, I was born too practical, an old woman even at a young age. I had no time for nonsense. And third," the woman leaned closer to Dulcie and said *sotto voce*, "she was crazy as a bat!"

Dulcie burst out laughing. The sound rang in the otherwise silent room. She held out her hand. "I'm Dulcie Chambers. I'm here from the States."

The woman held out her hand as well, beautifully dark with a simple yet perfect sapphire and gold ring on it. She shook Dulcie's hand. "I am Cassandra Watts, a volunteer here at the Bermuda National Gallery. However, I believe that you are more than just *from the States* Ms. Chambers? You see, I've always kept up with my studies. Dr. Dulcinea Chambers is the director of the Maine Museum of Art. Would you be the same Dr. Chambers, or is this an amazing coincidence of mistaken identity?"

"You're right, I confess. No coincidence. I'm going a bit incognito at the moment as a quick break." Dulcie sighed, trying to put thoughts of her situation at home out of her mind. "As you must know, however, if this," she waved toward the paintings, "is in your blood, it's impossible to take even a quick break."

Cassandra smiled. "You are right. When I travel I must see the museums wherever I go. But tell me, does this exhibit interest you, or simply the museum in general?"

"I'll be diplomatic and say 'the museum' but between the two of us, I'm very interested in this exhibit. Botanicals have always fascinated me. I think it's the cross between science and art, and possibly even a bit of historical witchcraft thrown in for good measure." Dulcie looked back at the painting on the wall. *Convolvulus.* Morning glory. She had seen variations of them so many times growing wild back in Maine.

Cassandra looked over at the painting as well. "Yes, the balms and teas of herbal healers long ago. I think that with all of our pills and shots today, we have lost the effect of a good healing." Her blue eyes were the same color as her ring and sparkled equally as much. Dulcie could imagine Cassandra living centuries earlier, mixing potions and healing people with 'mystical powers.' As if reading Dulcie's mind, Cassandra leaned toward her and whispered, "My Aunties told me that I have witches in my ancestry!"

Dulcie's eyes were wide. "Do you think that's true?" she asked.

Cassandra shrugged her shoulders. "First one must believe in witchcraft. As for me, I believe in science," she smiled, then nodded toward the paintings, "and art."

Dulcie understood. Art. It was her salvation. The constant in a life that kept changing. She could always find herself again, stay centered in the confusion, when she walked into a museum and simply wandered through the quiet galleries. Sometimes she wondered if it was that feeling, more than any interest in history or the artwork itself, that drew her to the career she had chosen. She pulled herself from her thoughts realizing that Cassandra was speaking again.

"The artist here was a woman. I find that interesting. Lady Charlotte Anna LeFroy. Her husband was the Governor of Bermuda in the 1870s, and a scientist. She must have enjoyed science too, as these works are only a few of her botanicals. She did many paintings in Tasmania where they also lived. India as well, where she travelled with her first husband." Cassandra turned to Dulcie. "Don't you find it unfortunate that women of the past often led such exciting lives, yet it is the men that we hear stories of? We know little of Lady LeFroy. We must try to learn about her from her work."

Dulcie nodded in agreement. The morning glory vines curled and spiraled around each other like miniature corkscrews. They were so delicate. Dulcie could imagine Lady LeFroy concentrating hard, pushing aside the rest of the world, and using a tiny brush to create them. She would have been completely focused on her work, oblivious to anything happening around her.

That's what Dulcie wanted to do right now. Tune out everything else but her work. She turned to Cassandra. "I'm considering an exhibit of botanicals from around the world for my museum," she said. "I'm glad to find an example of a woman artist that I might be able to include."

Cassandra smiled. "As am I." She put her hand gently on Dulcie's arm. "You must let me know how you do with your work. I see great things in you Dr. Dulcinea." She squeezed Dulcie's arm gently as though she were a little child, then drifted off into the shadows of the next gallery.

Dulcie turned away from the final painting in the exhibit, pushed through the heavy glass doors and stepped lightly down the carpeted stairs. She emerged onto the wide stone steps that fronted the building. Squinting in the bright light she searched through her bag for her sunglasses. Only after a few moments of rummaging did she realize that they were still on top of her head.

She slid them down then looked around, trying to decide what to do next. This trip to Bermuda had been a lark. No, it was actually an escape. Her cell phone had at least five unread text messages. Fortunately they had stopped once she left the US since she didn't have international calling access. She did have email, however, and did not even want to check that.

Dulcie slowly descended the imposing steps. The late afternoon shadows were beginning to encroach on the street. Carefully looking in both directions several times — Bermuda traffic came from the opposite direction from what she normally expected — she crossed and made her way to the waterfront.

A ferry blasted its horn as it pulled away from the dock. She watched it for several minutes as it went across the harbor toward Salt Kettle. '*Dan would love it here,*' she thought. Her brother was back in Maine running his business of giving tours around Casco Bay on the small yacht that he and Dulcie had bought. Dulcie could imagine him doing the same thing in Hamilton Harbor.

Bermuda was the closest place that she could think of where she could truly run away. Nova Scotia had been a possibility, but geographically it seemed too much like Maine for her. The flight to Bermuda from Boston had been under two hours, but when she arrived she felt as though she was half way around the world. The water was a brilliant aqua. The houses, painted soft pastel colors with white roofs, looked like cakes with fondant icing. To her ear everyone spoke with a gentle accent, somewhere between British and a Caribbean lilt. She had laughed to herself thinking how flat and ugly her voice must sound to them.

Her passport was due to expire in a few months. A moment of panic had set in after she bought the non-refundable ticket, but had forgotten to check her passport's date. She had just made it in to the country under the pesky six-month rule. She had to remember to renew, just in case she needed to escape again.

There it was once more, that word: escape. Why did she need to escape? There really was nothing to escape from. She had never had a relationship with him. They had never really even been on a date. There was the one "thank you" dinner, but that was all. Yet she felt betrayed. Why?

Deep down, she knew why. Even though they had not been intimate by the usual definition, the fact that they worked together on two separate murder cases threw them together in a very intimate way. Dulcie tried to convince herself that they were simply working too closely. However, she could not deny that he had seemed to show more of an interest in her than was strictly professional.

But then, the bombshell. He was unavailable. Completely unavailable. He must have known it would affect her, or he would have mentioned it from the start. He must have known it *did* affect her, or he would not have seen any need to leave multiple text messages.

She was not going to let it bother her any more, however. She shook her head vigorously and walked on down the street. Nicholas Black would continue on the path of his life, and she would continue on hers. And hopefully those paths would not cross again.

 C8

Nicholas Black sat back in the uncomfortable wooden chair and looked around the conference room of the law offices that his grandfather had founded. He had just finished signing papers. The lawyer handling his case, the droning Robert Cavanaugh, Esquire, walked in the room as Nick put down the pen. "Ah, good. Perfect timing," he said in a nasally voice with pudgy lips that barely moved. "She'll contest again probably, but this time she can't stall any longer. We've got her." He tapped Nick's laptop with the eraser end of his pencil. The computer contained the critical piece of evidence, grounds for divorce that were irrefutable: adultery.

The first time that Nick had asked for a divorce, just after he had finished law school, she had laughed at him. The issue was money, of course. It had always been money. That's why she had married him in the first place, although he had been completely unaware of the fact. Stupid of him, in retrospect. They had known each other since childhood, yet she had never shown any particular interest in him then.

She had managed to stall the divorce proceedings on several occasions. Not content with a standard alimony payment, she was simply holding out for more money. She knew that when he reached the age of thirty, only several months away at this point, he would receive a huge trust fund. If they divorced before then, she would get none of it. But by dragging everything on until his birthday, she would then be entitled to half. Prolonging everything had little impact on her life other than requiring her to maintain a low profile. It was all lawyers' work.

Why had Nick married her? He sighed as Robert Cavanaugh, Esquire shuffled through the papers. Nick knew why. He was young. He was easily manipulated. He let his family rule his life. She was beautiful of course, which always affects the situation, especially for a relatively inexperienced college boy. She had also done everything in her power to entice him. That is, until the day after the wedding, which had taken place the day after his graduation from Harvard. That's when it all began to change.

Nick had not recognized it immediately, but their 'similar interests' quickly began to fade away. He had always enjoyed museums. She now found them boring. He liked to sail. She suddenly hated how the wind snarled up her hair. He liked to go to his family's quiet beach house and spend the evenings reading a good book. She now preferred to stay in Boston and go out at night with her friends.

When he mentioned his troubles to his parents, their response was decisive. "Make it work. Besides," his father had said, "when you become a lawyer and join the firm, she'll be an asset." Nick didn't want an asset. He wanted a friend. He wanted a companion. He wanted a wife.

He had been in law school for two years and was facing the bar exam. He had taken to closing the door of his study for hours so that he could review for it. In fact, he had not been studying. He had been doing nothing but stare at the walls and wonder how to get out of the mess that his life had become. As the day of the exam drew nearer, he knew that he was not ready.

He also knew that he had never intended to take it in the first place.

His link to Robert Cavanaugh, Esquire had begun as a class project in law school. Nick had been researching a case and his father, now retired, had suggested Cavanaugh as a good source of information. Of course the younger lawyer could not refuse to help the son of a senior partner and grandson of the firm's founder.

The relationship between Cavanaugh and Nick could not exactly have been termed a friendship. It was more of a mutual understanding. Cavanaugh was many things, but stupid was not one of them. He quickly realized that Nick's questions did not exactly pertain to the case that he was studying. Cavanaugh knew that they were of a more personal nature. He sympathized with the young law student. Robert Cavanaugh, Esquire had been used for his money too, and had also experienced some difficulty extricating himself from his own situation.

Now Robert Cavanaugh, Esquire looked across the table at Nick. "Yep, you've got her this time. And not a moment too soon as you're well aware." The final word hummed through his nose. "I'll get this through as fast as I can."

Nick nodded. He would have smiled, but he found no pleasure in any of it. He was tired, drained. "Thanks, Bob. You don't know how much I appreciate this. I know it's been tough, especially with my father not exactly supportive."

Cavanaugh waived his hand quickly over the table, as if to clear away the invisible dust in the air. "He's retired. The rest of us are in charge now. Besides, he doesn't know what it's like to get hosed. Or at least, I don't think he knows."

This time Nick did smile, although ruefully. "No, I don't think he does." His parents had always been on the same team, putting family honor and pride before anything else. He had heard many arguments behind closed doors, but before the rest of the world they were a united front. Personal happiness, individual happiness, was irrelevant.

Cavanaugh collected the papers together, tapped the edges on the table several times until they were perfectly aligned, then stood up. Nick did as well. He stuck out his hand and shook Cavanaugh's awkwardly.

"I'll let you know a court date. And it will be *well* before your birthday, you have my word," Robert Cavanaugh, Esquire squawked through his nose. With that, he held the door open for Nick, who walked through it for what would be, hopefully, the last time.

෫

Dulcie returned to her room at the Hamilton Princess Hotel. She usually liked to stay somewhere near a beach so that she could swim, but this was a different sort of excursion. For this trip she just wanted to ride the ferry around the harbor, stare at the palm trees waving over the ocean, and of course visit the Bermuda National Gallery, an easy walk from the hotel.

Truth be told though, the biggest draw of the Hamilton Princess for her was high tea, to which Dulcie had happily succumbed the day before. When she was in Bermuda she had to restrain herself from having high tea every single day, which she could have, easily. '*Why don't we do this in America?* ' she had thought once again while eyeing the three-tiered plate stand. The waiter had carefully described all of the little sandwiches and treats, but Dulcie could not remember a single one. It didn't matter. They were all so good. She'd attempted to appear ladylike as she devoured them all while sipping tea and reading a book.

Dulcie found herself smiling as she thought about that lovely hour devoted entirely to food and fiction. Now, reality had come screaming back. She stood in the middle of her room and eyed her laptop as though it was the enemy.

She did not want to open it. There would be emails. Too many emails. And not just from him either. She reached beyond it on the table and picked up the bottle of wine that she'd grabbed at the duty free shop after her arrival. Bordeaux. A label that she usually didn't see in the States. She had spent too much on it and did not care. She had opened it the previous night, and it had not disappointed. Now she popped out the cork and searched around the room for a glass. Something that resembled a whiskey tumbler was in the bathroom with a little cardboard cover over it to ensure, somehow, that it was sparkling clean. Good enough.

She poured a glass of wine, took a deep breath, and opened her laptop. The messages began downloading. They kept downloading. Dulcie looked away, not wanting to see his name appear. She stood up and opened the door to the balcony.

With the gentle breeze fluttering the curtains, Dulcie at last turned to the computer. Oddly, there was only one message from Nicholas Black. It simply said:

> *Dulcie, I've been trying to get in touch via text. Just heard you were away. Hope all is well. I'd like to see you when you get back.* —*Nick*

That was it? She had expected more. Should she reply? She sat back and sipped her wine. Then she noticed the series of emails from Rachel.

Rachel had been Dulcie's assistant since Dulcie had become the director of the museum. Rachel had started out as a volunteer at the front desk but had proved her capabilities well. She had a way of being able to second-guess everything that Dulcie needed before she needed it. It was a natural fit, so when it was obvious that Dulcie needed an assistant, it was equally obvious who that person would be.

Now, however, it seemed that Rachel was in over her head. Dulcie started with the oldest message and worked her way up:

> *Visiting artist is here… not happy… needs larger place on ocean with north-facing studio… must have room for wife and sister as well… needs different brand of paint in museum studio, must order from France… will only work with maximum of five students for master classes… must have freshly brewed green tea from Ceylon…*

"Oh my!" Dulcie said out loud. She immediately wrote back:

Rachel, hang in there. I'll be back tomorrow and clear everything up. Sorry you're stuck with this situation. I had no idea! Thanks for all your work so far. —Dulcie

Logan Dumbarton. Noted for his abstract oils of seascapes. At least, most art critics assumed they were seascapes, and Logan never denied it. His sister was his business manager and had initially contacted Dulcie with the idea for Logan to come as a visiting artist. The sister and Dulcie had emailed and telephoned over several months, and Dulcie had believed that all of the plans were in place, which was why she had left his initial arrival in Rachel's capable hands.

For one brief moment Dulcie thought about calling Rachel. Then she decided against it. She would be back soon enough and perhaps most of the issues would resolve themselves. Dulcie did find it strange that there were so many concerns, though. The sister, Linda, had seemed perfectly capable, professional and reasonable. Yet she had never indicated that she would be coming as well, and certainly had never mentioned that her brother was bringing his wife. Or that he even had a wife. '*That must be a new development,*' thought Dulcie. '*I'm losing my touch. I used to know all the gossip about the big names.*'

She closed the laptop, firmly deciding against any reply to Nick. She really didn't have anything to say.

If you would like to read more of the Dulcie Chambers Museum Mysteries please visit the author's website (kerryjcharles.com) for additional information, or request copies at your local bookstore or library. Ebook versions are also available from major suppliers online.

Reviews from thoughtful readers are always welcome on any website or media outlet. Thank you!

ABOUT THE AUTHOR

Kerry J Charles has worked as a researcher, writer, and editor for *National Geographic*, the Smithsonian Institution, Harvard University and several major textbook publishers. She holds four degrees including a Master's in Geospatial Engineering and a Master's in Art History from Harvard University. She has carried out research in many of the world's art museums as a freelance writer and scholar.

A swimmer, scuba diver, golfer, and boating enthusiast, Charles enjoys seeing the world from above and below sea level as well as from the tee box. Her life experiences inspire her writing and she is always seeking out new travels and adventures. She returned to her roots in coastal Maine while writing the Dulcie Chambers Museum Mysteries.

Made in the USA
Middletown, DE
23 April 2020